P9-DNN-971

The Christmas Blessing

ALSO BY DONNA VANLIERE

The Christmas Shoes

The Christmas Blessing

DONNA VANLIERE

ST. MARTIN'S PRESS
NEW YORK

 For information, address St. Martin's Press, 175 Fifth Avenue, New York, N.Y. 10010.

www.stmartins.com

Library of Congress Cataloging-in-Publication Data

VanLiere, Donna, 1966–
The Christmas blessing / Donna VanLiere.—1st ed.
p. cm.
ISBN 0-312-32293-3
1. Physician and patient—Fiction. I. Title.

PS3622.A66C48 2003
813'.6—dc21

2003054763

First Edition: October 2003

10 9 8 7 6 5 4 3 2 1

For Gracie,

who proves the most priceless gifts come in small packages

ACKNOWLEDGMENTS

As always, my husband, Troy, was the first to read this manuscript and offer honest, sometimes painful, feedback. Thank you, Troy, for constant encouragement. Your enthusiasm is contagious.

We loved our daughter, Gracie, in our hearts long before they put her in my arms when she was ten months old. Thank you, Gracie, for your joy, happiness, imagination, laughter, smile, "Elmo–Pooh Bear–blankie," dances, "big hug," and kisses.

I made many eight-and-a-half-hour trips to northeast Ohio so my parents could baby-sit while I worked. It was a long way to drive for child care, but I always knew Gracie was loved and cared for. Mother and Pop, thank you for all the good food and the many days you gave us.

My agent, Jennifer Gates, always believes in my work and makes the journey of writing enjoyable. Thank you, Jennifer, for being able to see past rough outlines or fragmented chapters to catch my vision, however dim it may be at the time, and make it stronger. Thanks also to Esmond Harmsworth for his time and feedback, and to everyone at Zachary Shuster Harmsworth.

Jennifer Enderlin, my editor, encouraged me to write a sequel to *The Christmas Shoes* and provided invaluable guidance. I appreciate your work and the belief you have in this book, Jennifer. Many thanks also to John Karle and to the St. Martin's sales staff for making calls and pounding the pavement on behalf of this book.

Beth Grossbard is petite in stature but big on vision and belief! Thanks, Beth, and thank you, Craig Anderson, for making dreams and ideas reality.

Great thanks to Byron Williamson, Rob Birkhead, Derek Bell, and the staff of Integrity Publishers for all your work and effort in the CBA marketplace.

Three physicians helped me get this manuscript into shape. I couldn't have done it without their help. If there are medical mistakes in the book, the fault is mine, not theirs.

We met Dr. Skip Hagan in China while he and Melissa were adopting Janie. Although he was busy with three children and Emergency Department duties, Skip always had time for my medical questions. Thank you, Skip, but most of all, thanks for the friendship with you and Melissa.

Jackie Russell put me in contact with Dr. Ann Kavanaugh-McHugh with Vanderbilt Children's Hospital Division of Pediatric Cardiology. Thanks, Ann, for generously sharing your knowledge with me and helping with everything from a heart patient's diagnosis to treatment. Thank you, Jackie!

My cousin, Paula Ross, introduced me to Dr. Anne Wilkerson, who provided rich insight into her years of medical school and rotations. She was a tremendous help in making each medical scenario in the book realistic and believable. Your help was invaluable, Anne. Thank you, Paula!

Sandy Ivey guided us through our first adoption and is gently leading us again. Thank you, Sandy, for helping us bring our babies home! We couldn't do it without you.

I wrote much of this book at the Medina County District Library in Ohio. The staff was always kind, helpful, and, of course, quiet. Thank you all.

I'm blessed to know people, many of them teachers, who have consistently aimed for excellence in their work. They have inspired, motivated, or challenged me throughout my life. Thank you to Tim Cook, Wes and Rebecca Baker, Paul Dixon, Dorothy Elrick, David Foster, Jim Leightenheimer, Diane Merchant, Jim Phipps, Rick Powers, David Robey, and Jon Skillman.

Thanks to Eve Annunziato, Jenny Baumgartner, Jeff Brock, Eddie and Terri Carswell, Debbie Cook, Rebecca Dorris, Dave and Judy Luitweiler, Will Marling, Barbara McGee, Cheryl Reese, Tammy Rich, Peggy Rixson, Peggy Starr, Laurie Whaley, and Vince and Sharon Wilcox for your encouraging spirits, kindness, and for taking the time to be friends.

And, again, thank you to Bailey, who never left my side when I worked and was the first to remind me when it was time to lighten up and take a walk.

We are built for the valley, for the ordinary stuff we are in,
and that is where we have to prove our mettle.

—Oswald Chambers

PREFACE

December 24, Present Day

It's Christmas Eve, and the lake in front of me is frozen hard. Snow surrounds the edge, crunching beneath my feet. The sun is beginning to sink, and the trees, heavy with snow, cast long shadows over the paved path that runs along the shore. Several runners make their way around the perimeter, careful not to bump into the occasional walker on the inside of the path. I stand for a few moments in that familiar spot, beneath the giant oak tree, looking out over the smooth surface. As I'd driven through the icy streets on my way to the park, past familiar shops and sights, I'd noticed few changes in the three years since I'd been gone. I take a deep breath and exhale, leaving faint clouds in the winter air. *I have work to do.* I open the tailgate of my truck and grab the legs of the heavy wooden bench that I'd loaded earlier.

When I was a boy, my father would wake me early on Saturday mornings, and we'd drive to a lake, much larger than this one, on the outskirts of my hometown, and push our tiny rowboat into the water. We'd always start before dawn. At the lake, we'd row out to our favorite spot and prepare our rods for a morning of fishing. Together we'd sit in silence and wait for the slightest tug on our lines. Often, we'd speak in whispers. My father was convinced that even the smallest noise spooked the fish, but when my father did speak, he'd say, "Be patient, Nathan. One will come," or "Be still, Nathan. Be still."

At the end of the day, we'd row back with our catch—we threw back more than we ever kept—and then, as we approached the shore, my father would sometimes tell me about his hopes and dreams and ask me about mine. "Even God's smallest plan for us is bigger than any dream we could ever hope for," my father said one morning, pulling the boat onto dry land.

I don't know why I have always remembered that moment; maybe I recall it because there was a time when I was a boy that I'd prayed for a miracle that never came, one that would have kept our family intact and saved my mother's life. I was eight years old when she died of cancer during the first morning hours of Christmas Day. Earlier in the evening I had run to Wilson's Department Store and bought her a pair of shiny beaded shoes. Looking back, I know they were gaudy and awful, but in my child's mind I thought she'd look beautiful as she walked into Heaven wearing them. I didn't know my mother would die that night, and as I climbed into bed and pulled the blankets high around my neck, I prayed again for a miracle.

As I helped my father pull our boat onto shore years later, I wondered how he could believe that God's plan for us was greater than anything we could have ever imagined if God wouldn't send a miracle when we needed it most?

A year earlier, I went with my mother one winter morning to visit my grandparents, who lived high on a hillside. We drove up the winding road that led to their home, and because the trees were naked, as I looked over the bluff at the top, I could see into the valley below. It looked so different from above, not as immense as I'd thought. We got out of the car, and my mother took my hand on that cold, windy day and looked down into the valley with me. "I liked it better looking up," I said to her. "Everything's too little from here." She knelt beside me and drew me close to her side.

"Time in the valley will teach you to be a man, Nathan. It's where your character will form." I looked down the slope and back to my mother. I didn't understand how roaming around in the valley below would help me to become a man. She laughed when she saw my puzzled face and stood up, taking my hand again. "You can only see small things when you're on top of a mountain. Do you know what I mean, Little Man?" I shook my head. *No, I didn't.*

She knelt in front of me and held my face in her

hands. "One day you will, I promise. But I hope you don't go straight to the top of the mountain, Nathan. I hope you go through the valley first so that you'll learn how to love and feel and understand. And when life wounds you, I hope it's because you loved people, not because you mistreated them." I didn't understand anything my mother was saying. She smiled and kissed me. "Always remember that regardless of what happens, Nathan, in the end there will be joy. I promise." As odd as it sounded, I've come to realize that it was her heart's cry for my life, spoken not necessarily to me, but for me.

People talk about a defining moment in life. I've come to realize that there is no one defining moment, but instead a series of events and circumstances that define who we are. They change us little by little, leading us to something bigger or unexpected or maybe to a closed door, and that is when we experience a grand moment of realization that drives us closer to our destiny. The times with my father on the lake and with my mother overlooking the valley are two such moments.

Today, I know that each of us is destined for something, a purpose that often seems muddy, or vague at best. We want nothing more than to know what our purpose is, to know that we haven't just been plopped down to fumble our way through to the end, but that there's a reason for our being here. We may not discover that purpose in the way that we'd want, as time in the valley will be longer and darker than we imagined, but if we are patient or still long enough, we will catch it in fleeting glimpses. We will see tiny sparks of revelation that push us closer and closer to our destiny. There will be pain; sometimes more than we bargained for, but as my mother promised so many years ago, in the end there will be joy.

ONE

Late October 2000

All change is a miracle to contemplate;
but it is a miracle which is taking place every instant.
—Henry David Thoreau

I gunned the engine, pulled the truck out of my parking space, and flew over the speed bumps on my way out of the apartment complex. A young mother grabbed her toddler and gave me a dirty look. I thumped the face of my watch, and the second hand seemed to groan before deciding to move. *Too late now, I'll never make it*, I thought, glancing at the clock in my dashboard.

I couldn't believe it; I was never late. I'd noticed that my watch was having problems a couple days earlier and had been relying on an extra clock in my bathroom to make sure I was showered and out the door on time. As I was shaving I must have accidentally pulled out the cord just enough to stop the clock from running. The tires squealed as I pulled out onto the main road, and the gardener working at the entrance to the complex gave me my second nasty look of the morning, even shaking his head for effect.

If I made all the stoplights through town, I could get to the hospital in fifteen minutes. Turning into the hospital lot, I glanced at the clock—fourteen minutes—a new personal record. There was no time to circle for a spot, so I parked at the far end of the lot and ran for the main entrance. *Maybe he hasn't started yet*. Who was I kidding? Dr. Goetz never failed to start on time. I ran faster between the rows of cars.

As part of my third-year medical rotations, the university had placed me under the tutelage of Dr. Crawford Goetz—the best cardiologist in the hospital. Cardiology wasn't part of a normal rotation block, but the university felt that a rotation in cardiology would only enhance a student's studies. So, I was stuck for the next four weeks with Dr. Goetz. He was a Harvard and Vanderbilt man, the chief of cardiology, father of four, grandfather of two, and a thorn in my flesh. He specialized in pediatric cardiology, but since the hospital had only a small number of child patients a year, as department head, Dr. Goetz would also oversee the treatment of adult patients.

In each of our rotations, a medical student was part of a team that consisted of an attending physician, three to four students, and an upper-level resident. Peter Vashti was the upper-level resident on Dr. Goetz's team. My clipboard with the day's rounds was hanging at the nurses' station, the last to be picked up. The other students and Peter were already following Dr. Goetz from room to room. I checked the room number for the first patient to

be seen and ran to catch up, sneaking in behind William Radcliff, an old friend and fellow student who, to my good fortune, stood six-five. Dr. Goetz was sitting on the patient's bed, a forty-seven-year-old man recovering from open-heart surgery.

"She's working like a thirty-year-old's heart," Dr. Goetz said.

"Does that translate to the rest of his body?" the man's wife asked, cracking a wad of gum. Dr. Goetz laughed. He had a carefree, easy way with his patients and their families; too bad that didn't translate to his students.

"So everything feels normal?" Dr. Goetz asked, resting his hand on the patient's shoulder.

"He's cranky again," the wife said, her gum exploding like a firecracker.

"Is that good or bad?"

"I don't know if it's good or bad, but for him it's normal," his wife continued.

The patient looked sheepish. Poor guy, no wonder he had heart surgery. She was relentless.

"All right, Jason," Dr. Goetz said, smiling. "You're ready to go home." The man shook Dr. Goetz's hand and I could see his eyes fill with tears; he started to speak, then stopped. He didn't want to get emotional in front of a handful of medical students. He pumped Dr. Goetz's hand again, nodded, and looked down at the sheet resting on his lap. Dr. Goetz squeezed his shoulder and turned to leave, nodding for us to follow.

⁂

Filing back into the hallway, we could hear Jason's wife get an early start on what could be heart attack number two. "What do you mean you're not going to wear the piece? Just because your heart's working again doesn't mean your hair's going to grow back. Put this on. Put this on, or I'm not walking out these doors with you. I mean it. I will not walk out these doors." For the sake of his heart, I hoped his head would shine like the new dawn as he left the hospital.

"Who's our next patient," Dr. Goetz asked, scribbling something onto Jason's chart. "Andrews?"

I looked down at the chart in my hands. "The patient in room 2201."

"Mr. Andrews," he said, as if giving a speech to a room of five hundred. "Just as you were not given a number at birth, but a name, you will find that your patients came into the world in the exact same manner. Learn *who* they are, not *where* they're located."

I could feel sweat break out on my upper lip. I never intended to seem demeaning toward the patient. "I didn't mean it that . . ." I began, but it was too late. Dr. Goetz had already learned the name of the patient and was leading the students through the halls.

"And Mr. Andrews, as a reminder, your rotation begins at six A.M. Not six eighteen." I felt my chest tighten. I should have known that Dr. Goetz would pick up on my tardiness.

During a break in rounds, I retreated to the lounge and sank into the sofa. I leaned my head against the wall and rubbed my temples. If I'd known there was going to be someone like Dr. Goetz in my future, I never would have signed up for medical school in the first place. I glanced at my watch and noticed it had stopped running again. I tapped the face, but the second hand wouldn't budge. I took the watch off and flipped it over to thump the battery casing. I ran my finger over the inscription: *With all the love in the world, Mom.*

My mother died about a year after she stood with me on the hill overlooking the valley. Maybe she knew she'd never see me grow up; perhaps she was preparing me for the long valley I would go through without her, or maybe preparing her family and herself for death was the final step of faith she would take.

I remember my father coming into my room during the early morning hours of that Christmas. He said that my mother had stepped into Heaven. He let my sister Rachel sleep; she was much too young to understand what was happening anyway. I ran to the living room, where my mother lay still on the hospital bed; my grandmother was holding her hand, weeping. I watched my mother for the longest time, praying she'd move again, that she'd reach for me and say, *You need to get back into bed, Little Man,* but she couldn't reach for me, and I knew it. She was thirty-four years old.

Wilson's Department Store was about to close on that Christmas Eve as I ran from one department to the next looking for the perfect gift until the shoes caught my eye on a sales rack. I ran them to the front register and pulled a crumpled wad of bills and loose change out of my jeans pocket. When the clerk told me I didn't have enough money, I was heartbroken. I just had to buy those shoes for my mother. I turned to a man behind me, and, before I knew what was happening, he paid for the shoes, and I ran out the door for home. When I helped my mother unwrap the shoes, she held them to her chest and made me feel as if I'd just handed her Heaven itself. We buried her in them. I started leaving shoes on her tombstone again when I was sixteen. The owner of Wilson's somehow found a similar pair every year and ordered them for me.

During the last weeks of her life, my mother wrote a series of letters to my sister Rachel and me. In one addressed to me she wrote,

Dear Nathan,
I have had many joys in my life but none that have compared to you and Rachel. I always want you to know that I fell more in love with you every day. Please don't ever dread Christmas, Nathan, but remember to look for the miracles instead. It may be hard to see them at times but they will always be there because Christmas is the season for miracles.

She finished the letter and signed it, *With all the love in the world, Mom.*

I was helping my mother string lights on the shrubs outside our home the winter before she got sick when she first told me about the miracles of Christmas. "Jesus was born at Christmas," she said, wrapping a long strand around a juniper yew. "He left Heaven to live here." She bent over the back of the yew and tugged at the lights, stuck on a low branch. I pulled along with her, and together we continued wrapping the bush. "That's kind of like us becoming a worm and living in the dirt," she said, wiping her nose. "Love came down on Christmas, Nathan. That's the greatest miracle of all. That's the true blessing of Christmas and why it will *always* be the season for miracles." She stood back and admired her work, frowning at the tangled mess. "It'll look better when the lights are on." She dug into the box and pulled out another jumbled string, talking as she worked. "If you get too busy, you won't see the miracles that are taking place right in front of you," she said, replacing a blown light.

Before she died, my mother bought special gifts for Rachel and me; she wanted my father to give them to us on our sixteenth birthdays. Rachel got a gold locket and I got this watch—a flat, gold-faced Timex with a simple black band. The inscription was a reminder of something I'd always asked her.

"Is your love for me as big as Texas?"

"Bigger," she'd say.

"As big as the United States?"

"Bigger."

"As big as the *world?*"

"It's even bigger than the world! But if you combined *all* the love in the world, it might come close to how much I love you," my mother told me.

I'd worn the watch every day since my father gave it to me, as promised, on my sixteenth birthday.

Soon after my mother's death I told my father and grandmother that I wanted to be a doctor. When people asked what I wanted to be when I grew up I responded the same. I wanted to be a doctor so I could help people just like my mother.

Before I knew it, I was through college and into medical school. *What a tribute to your mother's memory*, an aunt would say or, *What a tremendous way to honor your mother*, an old family friend would comment. I felt the pressure mounting—people were counting on me to become a physician—my mother's memory depended on it. But after three months of rotations and watching people suffer and die, and now a week with Dr. Goetz, I questioned whether I'd made the right decision. In all honesty, when someone died it left me emotionally drained, and I was taken back to the morning my mother passed away. I felt as if I didn't measure up, that I wasn't cut out for it. I opened my eyes and realized I needed to get back to rounds.

Our team gathered outside the patient's room, and Micah, another third-year med student on our team, stepped forward and began to give the patient's blood pressure, pulse, heart rate, and the results of a heart test administered the previous afternoon. Micah was the "gunner" of our group—a med student's term to describe a fellow student who was always the first to answer, the first to volunteer for a procedure, the first to give stats on someone *else's* patient, and the first to get on other students' nerves. The term had been around long before we ever applied to medical school. William and I shot each other glances as Micah handed out Xeroxed copies of an article on angioplasty from one of our textbooks, one of at least twelve articles so far, all of them filed after our rounds in the nearest garbage can. William and I suffered in silence; it was all we could do, there was a gunner on every rotation.

Helen Weyman was the next patient on our rounds. She was a fifty-two-year-old woman complaining of chest pain who had a history of cervical disc disease. I had done Helen's workup when she was admitted to the hospital the previous afternoon. I went over her progress notes with the team before entering her room. It was customary that the attending physician took over once the group entered the patient's room; it was our time to stand back and learn, but I felt it was important to greet my patients first.

"Good morning, Helen," I said, standing at her side.

"I see your daughter was able to bring your knitting to you. Now you're not so bored, I hope." Dr. Goetz glanced at me. "What are you making?" I asked.

"A baby blanket for my next grandchild . . . number three. I've made a blanket for all of them. She's due in the next week or two."

I picked up the blanket and turned it over in my hands. "You've even got her name in here!" I sensed Dr. Goetz waiting for me to finish. "Let's go ahead and take a listen to your heart again this morning." I listened to her heart and felt for her pulse. I was taking up too much time. "Dr. Goetz would like to listen to your heart today as well." I moved away from the bed. Dr. Goetz took my place and examined her. As he did, he asked her about all her grandchildren, where they lived, how long she'd been married, and if she'd make him a pair of slippers. She laughed, and I watched as Dr. Goetz won over yet another patient. Before leaving the room I squeezed Helen's shoulder and told her I'd be by later to check on her.

I walked with William toward the cafeteria for lunch when my pager went off. I walked to Helen's room. The baby blanket was still sitting on her lap. Her daughter Mary, looking very pregnant and uncomfortable, was sitting in the chair next to the bed. "Is everything all right, Helen?" I asked.

She leaned forward and rubbed her hand over her lower back. "My back has been hurting."

I helped Helen into a more comfortable position. "You've been immobile longer than usual, and that may be putting pressure on those discs in your back. Does that feel better?"

She paused for a moment. "Yes, thank you, I think it helped."

"So you don't think it's anything serious?" Mary asked.

"No, it may be just some inflammation around those discs. But we should rule out any other possibilities," I said, handing the knitting back to Helen. "How much longer before this is done?"

"Just a couple more days, I think," she said, taking the needles in her hand.

I left her room and went to the nurses' station to discuss follow-up with the nurse on duty and to page one of the residents when Mary came rushing from her mother's room.

"My mother needs help!"

A nurse ran past me and headed to Helen's room. I followed close behind. I had just stepped inside when the nurse called in a loud, firm voice.

"Page, Dr. Vashti."

I stood in the hallway, right outside Helen's door, feeling helpless as Peter wheeled Helen to the OR. I was ordered to stay behind and attend to the other patients on the floor.

I finished my duties and ran up the two flights of stairs to the OR. As I threw open the door, I saw Peter waiting for the elevator.

"What happened? How's Helen Weyman?" I asked.

"She died a few minutes ago," Peter said.

It couldn't be possible. Helen was knitting a few minutes ago.

"What happened?"

"She died from ascending aortic dissection," Peter said.

The elevator doors opened in front of us, but I couldn't step forward; my legs were too weak to carry me. Peter stepped inside the elevator and held the door open for me. "Nathan?" I looked at him but couldn't respond. My mind was racing. If Helen died of ascending aortic dissection, it meant the pain she felt in her back was caused from a tear in the aorta, not her cervical disc problem.

"She told me her back was aching. I thought that the pain was attributed to cervical disc disease. I had just gone to the nurses' station to—" Peter nodded, cutting me off.

"Given her history, I would have thought the same," he said. I stepped inside the elevator and watched the doors close. The elevator stopped, and I followed Peter into the halls of the cardiology department. "Helen was a woman with a long history of back problems, Nathan. She was much sicker than any of us knew, and sometimes

there's just nothing we can do. This is one of those times."

I walked past the room where Helen had stayed, and a nurse was clearing away Helen's personal items. I leaned against the wall outside the door. It felt hard to catch my breath. I bent over, resting my hands on my knees. My mind drifted to my very first rotation. During that two-week surgery rotation, a twenty-seven-year-old was brought in after a car accident. His arm had been lacerated in the crash, nearly severing it. In an effort to save the arm and avoid any further nerve damage, the patient was rushed to surgery.

The surgery was proceeding well, until twenty-two minutes into it, the patient's heart went into failure and he died. It was the first death I had encountered, and it hit me harder than I'd imagined; intellectually I knew it came with the territory, but my heart wasn't prepared. My heart was with the family when they received the unexpected news; it was there as the phone call was made to the funeral home for final arrangements.

I stood in the operating room after the monitors were turned off and stared at the man's face, his hands, and his clothing. When he woke up that morning he had no idea that the jeans and pullover shirt he wore would be the last clothes he'd ever pick out; he had no idea it would be the last car ride he would ever take. I wondered what his last words were to his wife or what he had said to his

mother or to his children. Did he have children? Even after the curtain was pulled around his body, I went back in and looked at him. It was hard to sleep for days. To make matters worse, I didn't see any of the other students suffering in the ways I did.

After Helen died, I confided my doubts to William during a game of one-on-one basketball.

"It's because our hours are so long," William said. "We've been thrown into the deep end, and we're going to sink or swim now. You'd see things differently if you just weren't so tired." He sank a shot over my head. I grabbed the ball and held him off with one arm. "You're taking Goetz too personally. He comes down hard on everybody." I ran around him and jumped in the air, aiming for the basket. The ball dropped through the hoop and William grabbed it, dribbling it close to the floor.

"It's not Goetz," I said, lunging for the ball. "A patient died under my care."

"She wasn't under your care. You were the med student on the team that was treating her," William said. He rested the ball on his hip, wiping his face with the back of his arm. "There was nothing anyone could have done. You need to stop blaming yourself." He was moving again. I charged for the ball and snatched it away from him, throwing in a sweet two-pointer. He caught the ball when it fell through the net and darted past me, up the middle.

"She trusted me, William." I wanted to tell him that

somehow I felt responsible for Helen's death, but I didn't know how to say it.

"Did you go into medicine thinking you could save everyone? If you did, you're going to burn out faster than any of us. What's important is that your patients feel safe with you. You're good with them. You know how to talk to them. Helen Weyman never thought for a second that she shouldn't trust you."

I wanted to jump in, and say, "Exactly! She felt she should trust me—that somehow I was going to help her but I couldn't."

"I don't think my patients like me," William said, moving past me, dunking another ball. I grabbed it and held him at arm's length.

"They're just afraid of you," I said, spinning on my heels. "You walk into their room, and they've never seen anybody as big as you. They're not sure if you're there to work 'em up or rough 'em up. You're an imposing black figure when you walk into a patient's room." I darted past him and jumped in the air. The ball swiped the bottom of the net and I groaned. William was ahead. He laughed and snatched the ball, dribbling it close to his body.

"You mean I'm like Shaft," he said, holding me away.

"You're badder than Shaft. You can insert a catheter." He laughed and tried to run around me. "Do you ever have doubts?" I asked, waving my arms in his face.

"Sure I do." He sank another shot over my head. I didn't believe him. But he was right about one thing: our

hours were brutal, the work was intense, and together they left me physically and emotionally exhausted. Now Dr. Goetz seemed determined to turn my rotation into the most miserable experience of my education. If I was going to start swimming, I had to get out of the deep end of the pool with Dr. Goetz before he drowned me.

Sleep never came that night. I looked at the clock at 10:30, 11:45, 1:20, 3:00, and then again at 4:45 A.M., when I finally decided to get out of bed. I stood in the shower for thirty minutes, hoping that the water would wash away Helen's memory, but every time I saw her face, I saw my mother's, and I just didn't think I could go through that over and over again.

Meghan Sullivan poked her head inside the hospital room of twelve-year-old Charlie Bennett. When the college freshman saw that the boy was awake, she ran to his bed and plopped down on top of it. "I looked all over for you after the meet. Your dad found me and said you were here. What's going on?"

"Ask Mom," Charlie said, eyeballing his mother. "She's the one who made me come." Leslie Bennett smiled as she stood to leave the room.

"He had trouble catching his breath, Meghan."

"It didn't even last that long," Charlie said, rolling his eyes.

"Only long enough to cut a few years off my life, that's

all," Leslie said, smiling. She grabbed her empty coffee cup off the table by Charlie's bed and left the room.

"How do you feel?" Meghan asked.

"I feel great. I didn't need to come in."

When Charlie was born, only one ventricle of his heart worked. He had three surgeries during the first three years of his life so the blood flow into his heart could be rerouted, flowing to the lungs without the aid of the other ventricle. The surgeries worked, meaning that the one strong ventricle supplied blood flow to his body and allowed Charlie to live a life like other little boys his age. He rested when he got tired, but nothing slowed Charlie down for long. He looked like every other child on the playground and preferred it that way.

It was only in the last five months that he'd begun to have any sort of trouble. "How'd you do today?" Charlie asked, sitting up in the bed.

"I came in first," Meghan said.

Charlie pumped his arm up and down with the enthusiasm of a coach standing on the sidelines of the Olympics. "What'd you run it in?"

Meghan looked down and smiled. "Fifteen-thirty."

The boy's eyes lit up, and he cracked his knuckles. "Man, I wish I could have been there! When's your next race?"

"Friday."

"Good," he said, giving her a serious look. "Cut two seconds off."

“What? Two seconds? Are you crazy? I already cut my old time. I ran the fastest I ever have today.”

Charlie brought his hands up under his chin and smiled. “Run faster.”

Meghan sighed. Charlie cracked his knuckles again and pointed his finger. “Don’t ever take your eyes off the finish line. If you take your eyes off the goal, you’ll never make it to the end.”

Meghan said the words along with him. “Never take your eyes off the goal! I know,” she said, shaking her head. “You tell me the exact same thing every time.”

Charlie turned into the stern taskmaster again. “Remember: two seconds.” Meghan stood and kissed Charlie’s face. He quickly wiped it off.

“Are you going to be there,” she asked, “or will you still be in here?”

“I’ll be there,” he said. “There’s no way I’m staying in here.”

Meghan had met Charlie her sophomore year in high school. Fascinated with runners he watched on TV in the Olympics, Charlie begged his mom to take him to the local cross-country and track meets. To Leslie’s embarrassment, the little boy would run alongside the runners, barking at them to run faster or keep their eyes on the finish line. He was quick to notice Meghan’s ability. “You’re the fastest girl I’ve ever seen,” he said after one meet. At each race, Meghan started looking for the little boy in the stands. She introduced Charlie and Leslie to

her family, and the two families had been sitting together ever since.

Meghan slung her bag over her shoulder and headed to the nurses' station, setting a clipboard on top of it. "Denise, would you mind if I left my sponsor sheet here so you could ask any of the doctors and nurses that I normally don't see if they'd like to sign up?"

Denise smiled and took the paper from her. She was well aware of what Meghan was doing; her name was already one of the first on the sheet. Meghan was organizing a run that would raise money for a pediatric heart patient fund. The money would go into a trust and be awarded each year to a pediatric heart patient as part of a college scholarship once the patient had been accepted to a college. "If they don't sign up, I'll inject them with some sort of sponsor-sheet injection drug we must have around here someplace," Denise said, looking in the drawers.

I walked toward the nurses' station and was looking over the notes on my clipboard when a young woman ran into me, knocking it out of my hands.

"I'm so sorry," she said, swooping the clipboard up before I could get to it. She laughed, and her blue eyes sparkled. Her light brown hair fell just on top of her shoulders, and when she smiled, her face lit up. She was lovely.

"No, no. It's my fault," I said. "I shouldn't have been walking on the side of the hall that's clearly designated for running." She laughed harder, handing me the clipboard.

"Just keep that in mind from now on," she said, smiling, jogging toward the elevator.

I set my clipboard down on the nurses' station and rubbed my eyes. I could feel the pressure building in my forehead.

"Another rough morning with Dr. Goetz?" Denise asked. I groaned and peeked at her through my fingers. "He's the best there is. Really."

I folded my hands on top of the counter. "You know, everybody keeps telling me that. But those people have never actually worked *under* Dr. Goetz."

Denise shrugged her shoulders. "Just telling you what I've seen for years around here. People love him."

"Med students don't love him."

"Med students aren't people," she said, straight-faced. I looked at her and she broke out laughing. I noticed the sponsor sheet next to my clipboard.

"What's this?"

"It's for a scholarship run for the pediatric heart patients." She started typing into the computer. "Each year there's going to be a run to raise some scholarship money for college. The money will go into a trust, and when the patient is old enough and accepted into college, they'll receive a portion of the money as a scholarship and hopefully it will help pay some of the bills." She pushed the sheet toward me. "Do something good in the world. Sign up."

"Is this your idea of peer pressure?" She put the pen in my hand.

"You bet. Now sign up and help the kids."

"Who's the sponsoring organization for the run?" I asked, signing my name.

"It's not an organization. It's Meghan Sullivan. She's one of the fastest runners in the state."

"Is she on staff here?"

"No, she's one of our heart patients."

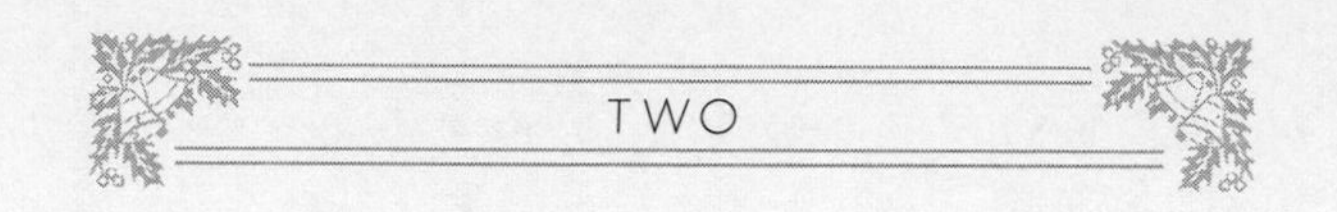

TWO

All happy families resemble one another,
each unhappy family is unhappy in its own way.
—Leo Tolstoy

Meghan was startled when the phone rang. She bolted upright in bed and stumbled through the dark hallway into the living room, where she picked up the receiver. It was Denise from the pediatric unit. Meghan's mother, Allison, crept up behind her and was able to make out bits and pieces of the conversation.

"What time," she heard Meghan ask. "How is she?" Allison watched as Meghan nodded and said, "Don't worry about it. We were up anyway," and hung up the phone. Meghan looked at Allison. "A heart is available for Hope." Hope Reed was a five-year-old who had been waiting for a heart transplant for six months. She had dilated cardiomyopathy, which meant her heart was enlarging, causing its ability to squeeze to deteriorate over time. An early-morning car accident five hundred miles away claimed the life of a five-year-old boy.

Meghan was quiet as she put on her running shorts and shoes and pulled her hair into a ponytail.

"I won't be gone long," she said as she closed the door behind her. The early-morning air was cold, and the sun was just beginning to break through the orange-and-red leaves of the trees. Fall was her favorite time of year to run. She went to a nearby park and started to stretch, looking for the runner with the neon ball cap. When she saw her, Meghan took off, speeding behind her.

Meghan pushed herself to keep up as the runner in the neon cap made one lap after another around the lake.

"She's like a gazelle," Meghan told her father one day. "I clunk around like a goat compared to her."

"It's because she's taller," her father said.

"No, it's not, Dad. It's more than that. There's a beauty when she runs."

Jim Sullivan held his daughter's face in his hands. "There's a beauty when you run, Meghan, and everybody around you can see it." Meghan dismissed what her father said. Of course, he had to say that, that's what fathers do. He put his arm around her and pulled her down next to him on the sofa.

"Why do you wait around for her every day?"

"Because she's the best runner I've ever seen. If I'm going to run, I'm going to run after somebody better than me."

The fall air was stinging Meghan's lungs, but she

pushed harder to keep up. When the runner finally slowed down and walked over the crest of the hill toward her car, Meghan stopped, breathing hard, and stretched her arms high over her head. "One of these days I'll catch up to you," she said toward the empty hill. "And then I'm going to *pass* you!" She sat down on the wet grass beside the lake and pulled her knees up to her chin. "Help Hope through the operation," she whispered. "Please let this new heart work." She paused, looking out over the lake. She rested there for several minutes, tossing tiny pebbles and acorns into the lake, and watched as small ripples spread out over the water's surface. She got up, brushed herself off, and ran home to help her mother get Luke and Olivia ready for school. Although most students lived in the dorms or nearby apartments, Meghan wanted to live at home for her first year in college.

At first I thought it was too cold for a run. I hadn't been a diehard since my college days, but today I decided it was okay and drove to the park. I stood by my truck and stretched my legs. In the distance I saw two other runners on the path, a young woman wearing tight black spandex and a neon ball cap who blazed around the lake, and another woman wearing a knit cap. I watched Neon Lady as she ran the perimeter of the lake; she was serious and focused. *No doubt a gunner*, I thought. *A gunner runner*. But she was a great runner, all fluid motion when she breezed around the path, but then I noticed the young woman running behind her; she was pacing herself against Neon Lady. *That's what it looks like when you're doing what you're supposed to do,* I thought, watching them. They finished their run before I started mine. I walked toward the lake to begin my run when the young woman with the knit cap sat beneath the giant oak tree by the lake. *Probably routine for her,* I thought. *Runs her body hard, then clears her mind for the rest of the day.* It was something I should have done, but instead I finished my run, then jumped back into my truck and drove to my apartment. I had to get to the hospital.

I arrived at the hospital thirty minutes early to speak with Peter; he was the only one who carried enough weight to help me.

"I was wondering if I could possibly be part of another rotation." My voice sounded weak inside my own head, but I hoped it sounded convincing to Peter. He seemed a bit distracted, and I couldn't help but feel that things were already off to a poor start. He looked me over for a moment.

"But Dr. Goetz is a fine physician. I would say he's the finest at the hospital." I rubbed my temples. I couldn't take the "fine physician, one-of-the-best" speech again.

Peter took off his glasses. "Is this because of Helen Weyman? Because if it is, there will be other patients

who will die unexpectedly. The hospital's not in the habit of accommodating the wants of medical students, anyway. You know that." I sensed that the bomb was about to drop—there was no way Peter was going to pull me from this rotation.

"It's not necessarily a want, Peter. I need to change to another rotation," I said.

"Why?"

"Because I'm thinking of dropping out of med school, and if I stay under Dr. Goetz, I'm sure I will." There was a long pause. I hated putting Peter in the middle of my problem. He was supposed to be responsible for the med students on his team; coddling a student's emotional dilemma wasn't part of that responsibility.

"I'll see what I can do." I felt the weight of the world lift from my chest.

I looked at my watch; I had to get going. The other med students and I had to scrub in to observe a heart transplant for a five-year-old patient.

Meghan opened the door and saw Luke and Olivia eating breakfast at the kitchen table. "Was Neon Lady there?" Luke asked, as she stepped into the kitchen.

"She was there."

"Did you beat the pants off her?" Olivia asked, mashing the eggs on her plate into a fine, yellow mess. Meghan slid in next to her sister at the table.

"Nah, I let her win. I feel so bad for her. She's fast, athletic, attractive. How's she ever going to get ahead in this world with those kinds of attributes? If I didn't let her beat me every morning, she wouldn't have anything going for her."

After breakfast Meghan helped dress Olivia for school. "I can do it myself, you know," Olivia said. Meghan pulled a fuzzy sweater over her sister's head.

"I know you can, but I like to do it." Olivia sighed as Meghan tucked and pulled and straightened and buttoned her into her clothes for the day. Truth was, Olivia loved all the attention her older sister gave her. Meghan was more than generous with the time she gave both her sister and brother. Outside the bedroom door, Allison listened as Meghan and Olivia talked. To think that for so long, she and Jim never believed they'd have a family of their own. After seven childless years, Meghan was born in 1981.

Every night when Meghan was a little girl, Jim would carry her to the back deck and lift her head toward the stars. "That's the Big Dipper," he'd say, pointing, "not to be confused with the big dope . . . that's your daddy." He'd show her one constellation after another, then, pointing to a bright light, say, "That's what you are, Meg. You're a star. You're daddy's little star."

As he lifted her from the crib one morning, Jim noticed something was wrong: Meghan was lethargic

and nonresponsive. He was in the car with Meghan and backed halfway out of the driveway before Allison knew what was happening. She jumped in the car beside them and rode to the hospital without taking the time to put on her shoes.

The doctors took X rays and Meghan screamed; they drew blood, and she screamed louder. "You need to get her to a heart specialist," the emergency room doctor said. Jim and Allison were terrified. How could this be? The baby they'd tried so long to have was sick.

Dr. Crawford Goetz held the squirming child close to him and cooed in her ear. When Meghan looked into his eyes, a small smile broke over her face. "There's a hole in her heart," he said, gently running his pinky over Meghan's cheek.

"Oh my God," Allison gasped.

"However, it's an odd size. Normally, if the hole is too big, we go in and repair it. When they're small, we just leave them, knowing they'll eventually close on their own." Jim and Allison waited for him to continue. Dr. Goetz cradled Meghan in one arm, pulling her close to him. "I don't think this hole is big enough to repair."

"So it will close on its own," Jim asked.

"It may not close all the way."

"What if it doesn't? What will that mean?" Jim said.

"You'll need to monitor her activities, make sure she doesn't do anything too strenuous."

"But she can live a normal life," Allison said, taking Meghan from the doctor's arms.

"With restrictions she can. She might not be able to ride her bike as fast as the other kids in the neighborhood or jump in the pool twenty times in a row or run up and down the street playing tag, but it's too early to tell. We'll need to examine her throughout the years to monitor any changes."

Jim and Allison took their child home determined to treat her as a fragile gift, but Meghan rejected any acts of delicacy from the beginning. She loved to stand, balanced on top of her daddy's feet, and he would dance her around the living room, making her giggle and laugh with every spin. "Be careful, Jim," Allison would caution.

"She loves it!" Jim said.

"She might get too worked up."

But Jim would pick Meghan up and spin her till she kicked and bounced in his arms. If Meghan was sick, she didn't know it.

On her fifth birthday Jim and Allison took her back to Crawford Goetz, who took more X rays of her heart. For the last several years, the hole hadn't closed at all, but Dr. Goetz always beamed when he saw Meghan; she was proving him wrong, and he couldn't be happier. The child wasn't fragile and frail; she was a ball of fire. He listened to her heart through his stethoscope and smiled. "It sounds strong."

After school, Meghan would hop on her bike or run up and down the street with the neighborhood children. Allison would watch through the window from inside, rocking from one foot to the other, and chewing the inside of her mouth.

"Let her be," Jim would always say.

"What if something happens to her, and we don't see her fall," Allison snapped back, craning her neck to see Meghan through the window.

"She has to play, Allison. We have to let her play."

"The doctor said we'd need to monitor her."

"He didn't say to obsess over her." Allison moved from the window, pretending to busy herself around the house, but she always kept an ear tuned for Meghan's voice.

In second grade, after her parents had given up hope of having more children, Meghan became an older sister when Luke was born. Four years later, Olivia was born. When Meghan was in the third grade, the Sullivans moved to a larger house to accommodate their growing family. Their new home was situated on the other side of the city, in a different school district. Meghan was distraught over the move. She was moving away from her friends and beloved teacher. "Meghan," Allison said, tucking her in bed one night, "just think about all the new friends you're going to make."

Tears filled Meghan's eyes. "I don't want new friends."

"But you don't know who you're going to meet

there," Allison said, stroking her daughter's hair. "This could be the best thing to happen to you. This one little move will change all our lives. You just wait and see." The little girl nodded, telling her mother she understood. But when Allison left, Meghan cried herself to sleep, thinking of the friends she would be leaving behind.

Instead of riding the bus like she used to, Meghan became a "walker." Allison walked with her those first several weeks, pushing Luke in the stroller. "You can't walk her every day," Jim said. "We have to let her walk with the other kids."

So the next day, Allison helped Meghan with her backpack and sent her out the door for her first solo walk to school. But Meghan didn't make friends on her walk that morning and found none at school, so when the final bell of the day rang, she ran down the stairs and all the way home. Meghan ran to and from school every day for the next three years. Of course, Meghan's running made Allison a nervous wreck, but Jim would say, "Maybe she was born to run."

"Not with that defective heart, she wasn't."

"Dr. Goetz said her heart is strong, Allison. Let her run if she wants to."

Allison couldn't deny that Meghan's heart was strong. It was stronger than any of them had ever expected: their sick little baby was an athlete.

• • •

After Meghan finished getting Olivia ready that morning, Meghan showered and dressed, pulling her hair into a ponytail.

"The meet starts at three, Mom," Meghan said, putting her books in her backpack.

"Look for us, right side, fourth row up," Luke said.

"By the foghorn man," Olivia added. So that Meghan could spot them with ease, the Sullivans sat in the same place every time for her races: fourth row up, right side, by the coach with the bullhorn.

I washed every inch of my hands and arms, then a nurse slipped the surgical scrubs up over my shoulders and slid gloves onto my hands. Dr. Kenneth Jonan, one of the transplant surgeons, would perform the surgery, with Dr. Barry Mann assisting. Dr. Goetz filed our team into the operating room, and we waited for the transplant to begin. When Dr. Goetz entered, he bent low to the girl's ear and whispered something, squeezing her leg. As third-year students, theoretically, we were prepared to participate on some level in the operation, but Dr. Goetz kept us from it, with the exception of handing the surgeon an instrument if he chose to ask us for it.

From time to time, Dr. Jonan would speak to us without taking his eyes off his work. I noticed that on several occasions, Dr. Goetz leaned down and whispered in the girl's ear. "Doing great, Hope. Everything's looking good." Hope's new heart was inside a plastic bag filled with a sterile solution, sitting in a pail of slushy ice water. I was drawn into the surgery in a way I hadn't expected. I saw the heart beating inside the girl's tiny chest and was so moved by the sight that my throat tightened. Dr. Jonan stopped her heart and removed it; it was swollen and dark red. He passed the heart to a nurse, and she set it on a towel, where we watched it pump several times before stopping altogether. *Unbelievable*, I thought. The new heart was pale pink and glossy. Dr. Jonan rolled the heart into Hope's empty chest cavity, and we watched as he connected the back of the heart first. After thirty minutes of stitching, the heart was in place. Dr. Jonan removed the cross clamp and we waited for the blood to flow into the coronary arteries that fed the heart and watched as it began to pump. I felt like throwing my hands in the air and cheering. It was the most remarkable thing I'd ever seen.

"Amazing," Dr. Goetz, said under his breath, watching the heart. "It just never ceases to amaze me." He clapped Dr. Jonan on the back, and I could see him smile through his mask. Dr. Jonan bent over toward the heart again and continued his work.

"Clamp." There was silence in the room. I glanced up and saw Dr. Jonan looking at me. He held out his hand. "Clamp." I looked at the instruments and was afraid I'd hand him the wrong one. "Clamp," Dr. Jonan said, looking at William. William stepped forward and handed him

the instrument, securing a better spot for the remainder of the surgery.

Dr. Jonan and Dr. Goetz had a focused, professional rapport throughout the surgery and it was obvious that the medical team also respected Dr. Goetz in a way I didn't. *Maybe he is the best*, I thought.

After scrubbing up, Dr. Goetz met with us to recap the operation and to answer any questions we might have. For a brief moment I looked down at my watch and realized it had stopped running again. As I gave it a couple of quick taps, I noticed that Dr. Goetz was no longer speaking.

"Am I boring you, Mr. Andrews?" I could feel the weight that had been released earlier with Peter fall heavy on my chest again.

"No, sir."

"I would only hope that your patients will have your undivided attention and you won't be so easily distracted when talking with them." He reached for a pair of glasses in his pocket and began cleaning them with the sleeve of his white coat. "May I ask if you feel this is your calling, Mr. Andrews?" I could feel the eyes of my peers on me.

"Sir?"

"Is medicine a calling or a responsibility for you?" I was stunned. I don't know if I was more taken aback because Dr. Goetz was embarrassing me in front of my classmates or because he sensed my apprehension. "If it's

not a question you've addressed yet, I would suggest that you do." Whatever positive feelings I'd had about Dr. Goetz during the surgery vanished in an instant.

At the end of the day I made my way to the parking lot. My truck was on the far end, and I didn't think I had the energy to crawl, let alone walk to it. "Why don't you make life easier on yourself and get a new watch?" William said.

"The watch isn't the problem."

"It was today!" he said, chuckling. I was glad someone could get a laugh from my misery.

"Is medicine a calling or a responsibility for you?" I asked.

He zipped his coat and smiled. "Hey, you're the one who's supposed to answer that. Not me."

I put my hands under my arms and walked faster to keep up. "What's that 'calling or responsibility' stuff supposed to mean, anyway?"

William shrugged. "I don't know," he said. "I think he just means that sometimes you act like you're becoming a physician because you owe it to the world." William stood outside his car. "Listen, when a doctor asks for a clamp, hand the man a clamp! You're not going to kill the patient, you know." He got into his car and started to drive out of the parking lot.

“So it’s wrong to care?” I yelled after him. “Is that what you’re saying? Doctors shouldn’t care?” He waved and squealed his tires as he pulled onto the road.

When Friday came, I couldn’t wait to get to my apartment and crash. On my way home, I drove past the university and noticed buses and cars lined along the street. The sign in front read, ROSS ROUNTRY MEET TODAY. In spite of my throbbing head, I laughed when I read it, wondering what the kid was like who made off with the missing “c’s.” On a whim I pulled into the drive. I parked the truck and made my way across the grass to the bleacher seats just as a pack of lean male runners grouped together at the starting line. At the sound of the gun, parents and classmates were on their feet, screaming and cheering. It was a large crowd for a cross-country meet, much larger than the spattering of parents who came out when I was running. As I looked at the crowd, I had to smile. My father, grandmother, and sister sat in seats just like these many years ago to watch me run against the best in the district, cheering till their voices were hoarse.

The race ended minutes later when a fine athlete from a competing school crossed the finish line in first place. A group of female runners walked toward the starting line, preparing for the sound that would send them bolting toward the woods and meadow beyond. As they gathered, a small girl in the middle of the crowd broke the

silence. She cupped her hands around her mouth and screamed something, but I couldn't hear what she said. Embarrassed, the girl's mother covered her mouth as the runners shot off their marks. A girl, tall and lean, her light brown ponytail tossing in the wind, blew past the other runners and took the lead. The crowd was on their feet shouting her name. I couldn't make out what they were saying, but it was obvious she was the hometown favorite, if not the competing universities' favorite as well. I got up and screamed along with everyone else. "Go, go, go!" I said with every step she took. I could see her wend her way through the woods, her strides long and fast. The other runners were pushing as hard as they could to catch up.

The crowd was so loud that I missed much of what the announcer said. All I heard as the winner crossed the finish line was, ". . . shaved three seconds off her previous five-K record. She ran it today in fifteen minutes and twenty-seven seconds." I'd never seen a girl run that fast—3.1 miles in just over fifteen minutes. No wonder the crowd was so big; the university had a star on its hands. I sat down and watched the crowd. I recalled that same frenzied energy from when I ran in high school and college. At the meets, I'd look up into the stands and scan the faces until I found my father, grandmother, and sister waving at me from the bleachers, my grandmother clasping her hands above her head and pumping them back and forth like a boxer taking the ring. I laughed at her and waved back, always wishing that my mother could be sitting with them. My head was pounding, so I decided against watching another race and headed home.

Michele Norris, one of the coaches for the women's team, caught Meghan and her family before they left the field. She was clutching a large brown envelope, smiling. "I didn't want to blow your concentration before the race," she said to Meghan. "But Stanford called me today. They've got a full scholarship with your name on it." Jim threw his arms over his head in victory. Meghan was too astonished to speak.

"That's the second school," Allison said. Georgetown had called a week earlier.

"I think there'll be others," Michele said. "I wouldn't be surprised if Colorado Boulder called. They all seek out the best and know that you slipped under their radar last year in high school. They know they're missing out on one of the best runners in the country." She put her arm around Meghan. "Now comes the hard part. Choosing." Meghan stared down at the envelope. Jim picked his daughter up, whooping as he bounced her up and down.

"They wouldn't even know who I am if it wasn't for you," Meghan said, between bounces.

"You do the hard part," Michele said. "All I did was create a little buzz."

Jim threw his hands into the air and whooped again,

this time picking Michele up and shaking her like a rag doll. "This is my problem," Michele said, grunting as Jim bounced her from side to side. "No single guys are ever interested in me, because married men keep picking me up."

Leslie Bennett drove Charlie to the hospital before Meghan's race. He begged his mother to take him to the meet, but his breathing was labored again so the race was out of the question as far as Leslie was concerned. Dr. Goetz admitted him for an overnight stay, and, once his medications were adjusted, Charlie fell asleep. Leslie stayed at his side. In recent weeks, she and Rich had noticed that Charlie had less energy and was sleeping more than usual. When Rich arrived at the hospital after work that evening, Charlie opened his eyes. "You can go home, Dad," he said. "I'm just going to go to sleep." Rich sat down and squeezed Charlie's hand.

"That's okay. I'll wait," his father told him.

Rich watched as his son fell back to sleep. He and Leslie had been overjoyed when their first son was born, at a healthy nine pounds. Even years after Charlie's surgeries he was still the picture of the active, normal child.

When Rich was dating Leslie, and in the early days of their marriage, he was in the Air Force, and like many service families they moved from base to base. When he left the service, Rich and Leslie moved back to where

they'd both grown up. That transition had been one of the most difficult of their lives. Unemployment was high, and Rich struggled to find work. He'd eventually found a job driving a truck for a local package delivery company.

Leslie resigned from her part-time day-care position within the last few months, when Charlie's visits to the hospital became more frequent, often leaving Matthew, Charlie's ten-year-old brother, with her parents.

Rich's job didn't provide the insurance coverage needed for all of the medical expenses, but it covered some, and anything helped at that point. Rich was taking any overtime hours he could get, hoping the extra income would help ease the burden of their mounting hospital bills, but there was only so much one man could do. The months of stress and worry were showing on both their faces. Leslie looked older than her thirty-five years. She had once enjoyed making herself up in the morning before heading out the door, but after sleeping on a bed no bigger than a cot by her son's side, makeup was the last thing on her mind.

Meghan walked to the nurses' station on the fourth floor. Claudia looked up from her files. "Charlie's doing great," she said.

"What happened?"

“He needed his medications adjusted. He’s fine now. Hope did great, too. She’s up in ICU.”

Meghan tiptoed into Charlie’s room. Rich and Leslie smiled, motioning her to come closer to his bedside. Meghan sat on a chair, leaning on the bed, careful not to disturb the maze of wires that were monitoring everything from Charlie’s heart, blood pressure, pulse, and oxygen level. She squeezed and patted his hand.

“I didn’t take two seconds off, Charlie,” she whispered. “I took three.” Rich and Leslie smiled as Meghan kissed his forehead. “I missed you, though. I couldn’t have done it without you.”

“Congratulations,” Rich said.

“When’s your next race?” Leslie asked.

“Thursday.”

“He’ll want to see you before then.”

“That’s what I’m afraid of!”

An hour later, Charlie strained to open his eyes. Rich and Leslie jumped to their feet and bent toward him, touching his face. “You’re still waiting,” Charlie whispered to his dad.

“I’ll wait forever if I have to.” It was something he and Charlie had been saying to each other for years now. When Charlie heard it, he smiled and fell back to sleep.

THREE

Most people run a race to see who is fastest.
I run a race to see who has the most guts.
—Steve Prefontaine

I was walking toward the lounge when I passed Hope's room. Since her transplant, our team had made sporadic visits to see her, but only long enough to check on her progress. Her mother, Beth, a part-time social worker, was always with her. Her room looked like a florist shop filled with flowers, balloons, and stuffed animals. Hope's father, Gabe, was a loan officer at a nearby bank, and many of his customers had sent gifts. I peeked through the window in her door to see how she was doing. She caught my eye and waved me in, her little body dwarfed by the tangle of tubes and wires and machinery surrounding her. Her eyes crinkled up when she smiled at me.

"In the middle of a so-so day, I know there's always Hope," I said, as if reciting poetry. Hope smiled and looked at her mother. "When people demand more of my time and I think I just can't give any more, I know there's always Hope." She giggled and looked again to

her mother. "When I need a pick-me-up but just don't know where to turn, I look for Hope." I stood at the side of her bed. "I don't know what I'd do without Hope in my day." Hope giggled, and her mother laughed, squeezing Hope's hand.

"Dr. Andrews," Hope said, "you're one of my favorite doctors."

"I'm not a doctor," I said, leaning toward her. "I'm a med student. It's this jacket. See," I said, taking it off. "When I take it off I look like an accountant." I put the jacket back on. "It's amazing, because people think they have to go through years of medical school and training to become a doctor when all they really need is a white jacket." Hope shook her head.

"No, you're a doctor," she said. "And you're my favorite."

"And I thought I was your best guy!" I turned to see Dr. Goetz standing in the doorway.

"You're both my favorites," she said, holding on to each of our hands. "But don't tell anybody else. They won't like it." Dr. Goetz put his finger to his lips as if he would keep her secret. I slipped from the room and walked toward the lounge.

"Are you on your way to see a patient?" I stopped when I heard Dr. Goetz behind me and turned to look at him.

"Uh, no," I said, unable to think fast enough. I regretted the words as they fell from my mouth.

“Good,” he said. “Walk with me as I check on Charlie Bennett.”

Great, I thought. I never wanted to be with Dr. Goetz as part of a group, let alone soak up some one-on-one time with him.

When we entered Charlie’s room, he was propped up in his bed, watching television. Two small blue ribbons were hanging from his hospital gown. Leslie sat at his side. Dr. Goetz stopped in the center of the room, opened his arms wide, and waited for a word from his young patient.

“It’s still beating away in there,” Charlie said.

Dr. Goetz walked to his bed and sat down. “Pain?”

“No.”

Dr. Goetz pretended to make a larger-than-life check mark on Charlie’s chart, which made Charlie laugh. “Breathing problems?”

“No,” Charlie said.

Two big check marks. Leslie chuckled at Dr. Goetz. “Sleeping?”

“Yes.”

Dr. Goetz pretended to make enormous exclamation points on the chart, circling his arm in the air at the end for a grand finale. I couldn’t help but be impressed by the banter between doctor and patient. Dr. Goetz listened to Charlie’s heart and took his pulse and blood pressure before placing an ankle on his knee, balancing the chart on his leg.

"Are they treating you okay," Dr. Goetz asked him. "Leaving a mint on your pillow every night?"

"They won't give me ice cream," Charlie said, annoyed.

Leslie laughed and rose to her feet. "I told them not to bring it. I didn't know if that should be part of his diet or not."

Dr. Goetz leaned in close to Charlie. "If I can get Mom to okay the ice cream, will you spend one more night with us so we can monitor how the meds are doing?" Charlie nodded yes, but everyone in the room knew that the boy would have given anything to go home.

A large, bearlike roar caught my attention on the television. I turned toward the set to see a wrestler body-slamming another wrestler to the mat. "Who's your favorite?" I asked, pointing to the screen.

"Ice Man," Charlie answered without hesitation.

I threw my hands in the air. "No way! Ice Man's all water. The Rock crushes him every time."

Charlie straightened up in his bed and stared at me, wide-eyed, cracking his knuckles. "Water turns to ice and freezes over rocks."

I shrugged my shoulders as if that were no big deal. "But then the ice melts and turns to water and guess who's still standing . . . The Rock!"

Leslie laughed. "Please don't encourage him."

Dr. Goetz rubbed Charlie's head and turned to leave. "Ice cream's on its way." Charlie waved, and I smiled, following Dr. Goetz into the hallway. "I didn't know you watched wrestling," Dr. Goetz said to me.

"I don't. The only guy I've ever heard of is The Rock."

Dr. Goetz led me through the hall as he made his way to the next room. "I've watched you with patients, Nathan; especially the children. You have a way with them, a natural ability that we can't teach." I could be wrong, but it seemed as though Dr. Goetz had just complimented me.

"We can teach you the clinical side of medicine," he continued. "But we can't teach personal care. Either a student has it, or he or she doesn't. Sometimes you tend to take that care a little too personally on yourself, but again, that's something we can work on." He crossed his arms and looked at me. "But I've watched how kids respond to you, and they already have a trust in you." He looked at me and paused. "Have you ever considered pediatrics or even pediatric cardiology?"

"No," I answered honestly.

"You might consider one of them, perhaps training with me in cardiology."

After those words, I didn't hear anything else. Dr. Goetz's mouth kept moving, but my mind couldn't process what he was saying. Long-term training with him was not even a consideration at that point.

"I'm being switched to Dr. Hazelman's rotation," I said, spitting out the words.

Dr. Goetz didn't falter. "Very good then." He tucked Charlie's file beneath his arm. "Let me know if I can

help." He disappeared around the corner, leaving me standing in the hallway. I leaned my head against the wall and closed my eyes. Was there even the slightest possibility that I was making a mistake? Maybe I should tell Peter I was wrong and complete my rotation with Dr. Goetz. I shook off the idea and walked toward the nurses' station.

The transition to Dr. Hazelman's rotation happened the next day, much quicker than I'd anticipated. He was part of the surgery block, which I had already completed, but his specialty lay in emergency medicine. I started with his team the last week of October and would spend the next eight weeks in the emergency room. I jumped into the work with both feet, anxious to prove to Peter and, maybe to myself, that I'd made the right decision in changing rotations.

On my first morning in the ER, we watched Dr. Hazelman perform an emergency gallbladder surgery. "Many women her age experience gallbladder problems," Dr. Hazelman said. "Why is that?"

"The four f's," Melanie, the "gunner" of my new group, said. "Female, fat, fertile, and forty. So, pregnant women are more likely to develop gallstones. Although this patient is not pregnant, she still meets the criteria." Dr. Hazelman nodded. Melanie clutched the clipboard tight to her chest and sighed, dazzled by her own brilliance.

Days later, a nurse directed me to a room where a sixty-six-year-old man was complaining of lower back pain. I was assigned to do his evaluation before a doctor saw him. I walked into the room, and the man was clutching his back, groaning.

"My name's Nathan, Mr. Slavick," I said, holding his chart. "I'm here to do your evaluation." He leaned forward to ease his back and groaned.

"Are you a doctor?"

"No, sir. I'm a med student."

"Get me a doctor now. I can't take this pain." I moved toward him to begin my examination but stopped. We had been taught during our first two years in med school that we were the main advocates for our patients. Sometimes the attending physician or the residents would be too busy to take much time with them, and that's where we came in, giving quality time and attention to the patient. We were told to be completely thorough in each of the evaluations we performed, but something was wrong here.

"I've never seen him like this," his wife said, wringing her hands beside me. I tried to listen to Mr. Slavick's abdomen but he grabbed my wrists, pushing me away, making it hard to hear through the stethoscope.

"I'll get a doctor," I said. I found Dr. Rory Lee, the fourth-year resident on our team, by the nurses' station. He followed me to the room where the Slavicks were waiting. "He's complaining of lower back pain," I said.

Rory put his stethoscope on Mr. Slavick's belly and felt his stomach with his free hand. Rory was pushing the gurney into the hallway and barking orders before I knew what was happening. I ran behind him.

"Call the OR. Tell them I have an abdominal aortic aneurysm about to rupture," he yelled to a nurse.

"Where are you taking him?" Mrs. Slavick asked, following us to the elevator.

"Your husband needs surgery," Rory said, pushing the gurney through the rush of people exiting the elevator.

"What's happening?" she cried as the doors closed.

A nurse approached me and stuck another chart in my face; I ignored her. I walked outside, stumbling over the curb. I sat against a wall and ran my hands through my hair. What a horrible day. I knew that someone would start looking for me, wondering where I was, but my legs couldn't lift me. Time passed slowly: twenty minutes, maybe forty. I'm not sure how long I had been crouched against the wall when Rory found me.

"Did he die?" I asked.

"No."

"I didn't hear blood rushing through the aorta."

"Because you don't have enough clinical experience," Rory said. "You can't read something in a textbook, then expect to pick up on it the very first time a patient walks through the door."

"Mr. Slavick was in pain," I said. "If I can't figure out why a patient is in pain, then I'm not doing my job. He

could have died. He *would* have died if you hadn't saved him."

"If someone's in pain, and we can't figure it out, or if a patient dies, it doesn't mean we're not doing our job, Nathan. During my ICU rotation in med school, I had four patients die in one night! I had two die last night in the ER. Sometimes bad things happen even when we do everything right. You have to let go of this idea that everyone is going to live because the fact is, people die. We apply everything we know to help our patients, but after that we have to let go." He looked to the end of the drive and watched cars pull in and out of the hospital. After a long pause, he said, "Have you ever considered taking a break from your studies, Nathan? Perhaps finishing your rotations at another time?"

It was one thing for me to admit to Rory that I didn't think I was measuring up. It was another for him to agree. "Maybe you should take a break and clear your head," he said. I sat speechless, my shirt wet with perspiration. "You won't be the first to do this. It happens more often than you know." I didn't know how to respond to him.

"What do you think, Rory?" I asked, but he just shook his head and looked down at the ground.

"I think you'd make an excellent physician, Nathan. You're smart, but you worry too much about getting an answer wrong. You're great with the patients, better than any of the students on this rotation, but you don't trust

yourself, and as a result you don't handle the pressure very well, and there is a lot of pressure when a patient is dying. But they do die, Nathan, and there's nothing even the world's best doctor can do about that."

I could hear myself breathing. "There's nothing wrong with what you're going through," Rory continued. "It might just be an indication that you need to step back. If you chose to break away right now, you would still have plenty of time to decide if this is right for you—to decide if this is really what you want to be doing—but I hope you don't do that." He stood to his feet. "I hope you're able to sort through whatever is clouding your thinking right now so you can move on to what I think you're meant to do."

He clapped my shoulder and walked back into the hospital, leaving me alone to wonder what I would do with my life.

That night, after flipping through seventy-plus channels on TV., I knocked on William's door. I figured that even if he'd already eaten dinner, a man his size wouldn't object to another meal. I was right. William was always up for food. We decided to walk to Macbeth's Pizza up the street.

"How'd it go in the ER?" he asked, pulling a knit cap over his head.

"Don't ask."

“Somebody vomit?”

“I wish that had been it, but you left out the urine.” William pretended to stumble from laughing. Macbeth’s was packed with university students, but I saw Melanie, the new “gunner,” waving to me from across the room. Melanie was the classic type A personality, always dialed up to ten; everything was much bigger than it needed to be. She was ambitious, gregarious, and obnoxious all rolled into one, and there was no way I wanted to have dinner with her.

“Pretend you don’t see her,” I said, looking in the opposite direction. But it was too late. We ordered our pizza and had a few moments of small talk before Melanie brought up procedures, patients, exams, and Dr. Hazelman. I wasn’t in the mood to talk about the hospital and was hoping William wasn’t either.

“Can you believe everything we’re doing?” Melanie asked. “Some days it’s staggering, but always accompanied by this adrenaline rush. Do you find that to be true?”

“It’s an adrenaline rush times ten,” William said, throwing all ten fingers in the air for exaggeration. I shot him a glance, and he smiled.

“I’m just amazed at what we’re learning and how I’m processing all of it, aren’t you?” I nodded again.

“I’m amazed at how smart I really am,” William said. I shot him another look, hoping to shut him down, but there was no way; he was having too much fun.

“Can I ask you something, Nathan?” Melanie asked.

“Sure.”

“Do you think you’ll ever make it through a procedure without breaking down in some way?” She laughed so hard I could see a dull silver filling in the back of her mouth. I felt the hairs stand up on the back of my neck. Our pizzas arrived and to my relief, William jumped in and changed the subject. He led the rest of the dinner conversation with a story about his grandmother, who served as a nurse during World War II, and how she amputated a soldier’s leg when no doctors could be found. The amputation lasted till we got our check.

“Thanks for saving me back there with Melanie,” I said, on our walk home.

“She’s harmless. Bags of wind usually are.” I started laughing, recalling William’s story about his grandmother.

“I didn’t know your grandmother was a nurse during World War II,” I said.

“That’s because she was a laundry woman in Philadelphia.” I stopped and looked at him. “Melanie’s not the only bag of wind you know. You need a good lie . . . I’m your man.” I walked into my apartment and lay down on the sofa, replaying what Melanie had said in my mind.

When my father and I would fish together on Saturday mornings he would sometimes get aggravated with me. I’d lean over the boat and play in the water, slapping the surface till it made a cracking sound. Dad, still speaking in whispers, although I’d been noisy enough to scare any fish within a ten-mile radius, would say, "Nathan, you either need to fish or cut bait." I knew I had to do that now. I either had to stay and finish what I'd started or get out of medical school and move on.

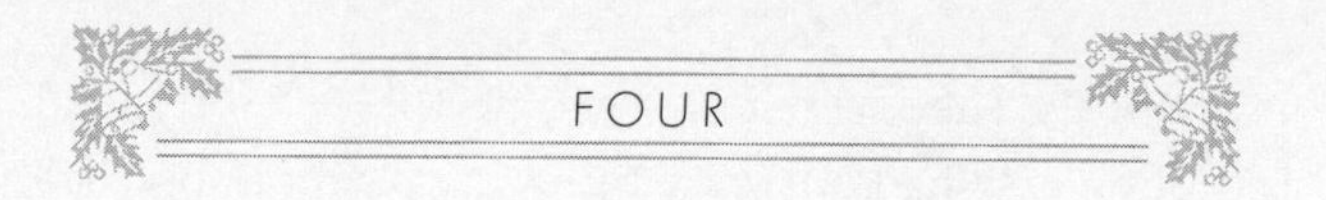

FOUR

No trumpets sound when the important decisions of our life are made. Destiny is made known silently.

—Agnes de Mille

I picked a cake up at the supermarket after work the next day. I'd ordered it that morning, a white cake with white frosting, yellow lilies, and *Happy Birthday Gramma* written across the top. Before my mother died, my grandmother had moved in to help with her care. She had been saving up for a cruise ever since my grandfather passed away and was planning to go with her sister when my mother became ill. She gave her ticket to another sister in Phoenix instead. "I don't want strangers taking care of Maggie," she told my father. "She's my daughter. When you're not home, I'll take care of her." She had taken care of my family ever since.

Lorraine, Gramma's best friend who lived up the street, met me at the door. She was wearing a bright multicolored nylon sweat suit, sequined with toucans and other tropical birds, and pink sneakers. She had struck up a friendship with Gramma when she'd moved in with us. They had soon become the best of friends, although they had only one thing in common: baseball.

Lorraine's team was the Atlanta Braves, although no one could understand why when there were teams that played much farther north and closer to home. Gramma's favorite was always the underdog—that, or any team opposing the Braves. Being in a room with Gramma and Lorraine while baseball was on was like watching a sitcom. If Rachel or I was there, Gramma would warn Lorraine not to swear in front of us. Lorraine would oblige until one of her men was called out, then she couldn't help herself. She'd start spewing words that would make Gramma explode.

"Don't swear in front of my grandchildren, Lorraine!" But Lorraine would be oblivious, letting loose on the umpires.

"Lorraine! The kids are in the room!" Gramma would shout.

At that, Lorraine would snap to attention and look at us, giving a sheepish grin. "Sorry, dolls," she'd say. We'd laugh and leave the room. And as soon as we did, we'd hear Lorraine screaming at the set again.

Lorraine kissed my cheek and eyed the big white box I was carrying in my arms.

"Why did you spend good money on a cake, Nathan?" Gramma asked, when I came into her kitchen. My sister Rachel was already home from college.

"Gramma, this is number seventy-seven. I think I can afford the fifteen dollars for a cake. It breaks down to just

pennies per year." A familiar smell wafted from the kitchen. "Is that lasagna?" My grandmother jumped to her feet, remembering something.

"Yes it is, and I better put a pan under it before the cheese melts over the side and sticks to the bottom of the oven." She made her way to the kitchen, her hip still stiff from a recent replacement.

"But lasagna's Nathan's favorite," Rachel said, "not yours. Shouldn't we be having something you like for your birthday?"

"I've been eating all my life," she said, sliding a flat pan beneath the heaping pan of lasagna. "I've had lots of opportunities to eat my favorites, but I doubt either of you have had a decent meal in weeks." She was right about that. I'd usually just grab something on the run. I began to set the table for dinner.

"Don't bother with that now. You two sit down," Gramma said to Rachel and me. "I want to tell you something." There was a glimmer in her eyes, a sparkle that told me she was up to something. She and Lorraine sat on the opposite side of the table, smiling.

"I'm setting your father up." Gramma slapped the table and laughed. "But the best part is he doesn't have any idea what I'm up to." Grandma slapped the table again, proud of her covert operation.

"Who is she?" I asked, curious.

She leaned toward us, whispering, as if the room were bugged. "Her name is Lydia, and I met her at church. She

has three grown children and a grandchild. Her husband died five years ago. Well, one Sunday Lydia came in and sat beside me and we started talking and she's been sitting beside me every week. She's on one side and your dad is on the other. The only thing separating them is me. But not for long!"

"What's she like?" Rachel asked.

"She's a gem. So nice." Gramma faded for a moment, thinking. "Sometimes people aren't so kind after they lose a spouse; it's too easy to get bitter, but she's a kind person, and so is your father. I don't know, but it just seems to me that two people like that should at least know that someone else like them is out there somewhere."

"Is she pretty?" I asked.

"She is, but not as pretty as your mother." No one was ever as pretty as my mother. "So here's my plan," Gramma continued. "Lydia is in the habit of sitting in the same seat every week. Your father's in the habit of sitting in the same seat every week. I'm always taking up that middle seat between them, so I'm not going to show up one week! Then Lydia will ask where I'm at, your father will say I'm under the weather, and before we know it, wedding bells will finally ring around here." The timer on the oven buzzed, and she jumped to her feet.

"I'll get it," I said, opening the oven door.

"Don't either of you dare tell your father what I'm up to," she said, squawking like a nervous bird behind me. "For once I'd like to keep something to myself around here."

I knew I should have told Gramma about the doubts I was having about med school, but I didn't want to worry her. If I told her I was thinking of dropping out, she would have conjured up the worst-case scenarios. She'd seen one too many television news shows. "You know, Nathan," I imagined her saying. "A young woman dropped out of med school and was gunned down in a strip mall parking lot. If she hadn't dropped out of school, she wouldn't have gotten shot," or maybe, "A man was found living with the winos down on the docks. Turns out he dropped out of med school." It was better to wait and tell my family when they were together.

When my father walked through the front door, I could smell the familiar scent of the garage; the scents of fuel and grease always clung to his hair and skin until he showered. He'd been working at the same garage, City Auto Service, and for the same men, the Shaver brothers, since before I was born. Carl, Mike, and Ted Shaver had been faithful to my father during my mother's illness and death, even paying him for days he couldn't work. Over the years he had been as loyal to them. Just as he never considered dating a woman, I don't think he ever considered finding another place to work.

I did my best to keep the dinner conversation focused on Rachel and off my rotation. I teased her about not bringing home a boyfriend to meet the family.

"And where are all those women who aren't standing

in line to go out with you," she asked. "That's right. They're out with other men."

"It'd be nice if somebody around here dated," Gramma said, eyeballing my father, who wasn't paying attention to her.

After dinner, we sang "Happy Birthday" to my grandmother. It was a pitiful rendition, two baritones and an alto in desperate need of melody. Gramma blew out the candle, and I placed my present in front of her. "Nathan, you shouldn't have spent your money on me." I rolled my eyes and cut her a piece of cake. Truth was I didn't buy it; I'd made it with my father's tools. Gramma ripped the paper and removed a small wooden box with lilies painted on the side.

When Mom died, Gramma encouraged us to write letters to her on special occasions: her birthday, Christmas, Mother's Day, but sometimes even the most insignificant details of our lives inspired them. Over the years, she used one shoe box after another to store them in, scribbling *Letters to Maggie* on the side of each new box.

When I was nine I wrote:

Dear Mom,
I've decided that my favorite snack is cheese. I loved E.T. and wish you could have seen it with me.

I love you
Nathan

One letter after another filled the shoe boxes. So often over the years, I'd observed the special care my grandmother took with the letters, even reading them in the quiet of her room. The wooden box brought tears to her eyes as she ran her fingers over the words on top, *Letters to Maggie*. She raised the cover and pulled a single letter from the bottom of the box.

I had written it earlier in the day:

Dear Mom,
Today is Gramma's 77th birthday. She cried when I gave her the present I made for her and then she cried again when she read this letter.
She loves you very much and so do I,

Nathan

Gramma laughed, wiping her tears with a napkin, then swatted me for making her cry.

When Gramma started to clean up the table my father stopped her. "Nathan and I will get these," he told her. "You and Rachel go in the living room." Gramma picked up another plate.

"You always get them," she said. "I'll get them tonight. Go visit with the kids." But Dad took the plate from her hand and led her to the living room, sitting her down in a chair.

“You cook. I clean. That’s been the deal for years now,” he reminded her. I smiled, watching them. It was a scene that had played out hundreds of times in this house. I scraped the plates into the disposal and handed them to Dad to load in the dishwasher. “How’s everything at the hospital?” he asked.

“Everything’s great.” He rearranged the plates to make more room in the rack.

“Now that that’s out of the way,” he said, taking the glasses from me, “how are things really going at the hospital?” He leaned against the counter, looked me in the eyes, and waited for my answer, an honest one.

“Did you ever think you should have done something else besides being a mechanic?” I asked.

He laughed and closed the dishwasher. “Every man thinks he should have done something else. Some days I’d have my head under the hood of a car and think of a hundred other things.”

“Why didn’t you do anything else, then?” He shrugged and started filling the sink with water and dish detergent.

“I don’t know. There were times I wished I could have had enough business sense to own my own place, but I wouldn’t have been good at that.” He rinsed a pot and set it in the drainer before taking a scrubber to a pan burnt with sauce. “For whatever reason, I can take apart a car engine. I don’t know why, except it’s provided a way for me to take care of my family, it’s given me steady cus-

tomers for the last hundred or so years, and I like to think that maybe the elderly folks or single mothers that come into the shop know I'm not going to take advantage of them. Maybe I was put there for no other reason than to watch out for people like that."

As I was growing up, the phone rang often at our house for my father: an elderly woman's car wouldn't start or a single woman was broken down at the side of the road. Dad would load his tools in the back of his truck and let me ride alongside him as he went to fix the problem. Many times he bought parts out of his own pocket. He'd shut the hood, wipe his hands, and watch as the stranded motorist drove off before we headed back home. I'd climb in the truck and look at him, wondering what in the world those people would have done without him.

"And if I hadn't been a mechanic, I never would have met your mother, so I guess there's a reason for everything." He wrung out the dishcloth before wiping down the counters. "Do you want to be a mechanic?" he asked, smiling. I shook my head.

"I'm not so sure what I want to be anymore," I said. I waited for the lecture. I waited for the you've-got-to-be-kidding-me speech, followed by arms thrown in the air. But it never came. If he was displeased, or worse yet, disappointed, Dad never showed it. He kept any advice or words of frustration to himself.

"Everybody's meant to do something," he said, assuring me. "You'll know what you're supposed to do; a moment will come, and you'll know."

"I think that moment has come," I said, dreading what I was about to tell him. Dad turned off the lights in the kitchen and sat in his recliner. I sat on the sofa next to Rachel, hoping I'd gain some level of support from her. "I need to get going," I started.

My grandmother jumped up and headed for the kitchen. "I've got Tupperware full of food from this week." She exited through the dining room and brought back four Tupperware containers, stacking them on my lap. "This way I know you're eating something good."

"Um," I said. Any conversation that begins with "um" is always off to a roaring start. I cleared my throat and started again. "Um, one of the residents talked to me yesterday." All three of them looked at me; they could tell by my tone that what I was relaying wasn't good news. "He suggested it might be a good idea for me to shelve medical school—to take a break for a while."

"What sort of crazy is he?" my grandmother snapped.

"He's not crazy. He's the resident for my current rotation."

"Why did he say that?" my father asked. I shuffled on the sofa; the Tupperware began to topple at the movement.

"Because something's not clicking with me, Dad. I don't know what it is." The room was quiet, with the exception of the television news playing in the back-

ground. My grandmother looked at my father, who, much to my discomfort, had never taken his eyes off me.

"But you still want to pursue medicine, right," he asked.

"I don't think so." I sat holding the Tupperware, hoping I didn't sound as dumb as I looked.

"You need to tell that horrible doctor that he's making you think awful thoughts about yourself and making you all crazy in the head," my grandmother said. She nodded toward my father, as if he was supposed to take over from there.

"He said he thought I'd make a good physician, Gramma."

"So what's the problem?" My grandmother was beside herself and threw her hands in the air. "People go through life wondering what they're supposed to do when it's always right in front of them. They should do what they're good at."

"But I'm not good at this."

"Nonsense! You're good at it all," my grandmother said, throwing her hands up in the air again.

"So this doctor is suggesting that you get out of medicine and do what?" my father asked.

"I could do anything: research, work in a hospital lab, maybe some sort of administrative position." My father nodded but didn't say anything.

My grandmother slapped the armrests and rocked

back and forth in her recliner. Dad wasn't handling this the way she wanted. "You were meant to be a doctor," she said. "From the time you were a boy you were meant for this." They didn't say it, but I knew my family was disappointed—I'd gotten this far only to drop out. We all stared at the floor, wondering what to say.

"This is what I think," my father finally said. "I think you need to fulfill your duties through the holidays. With Thanksgiving and Christmas coming up it seems much of the staff would be on vacation, and they would appreciate any help they can get around the hospital. Hopefully, during that time, you'll be able to think and figure out what you want to do." I'd have till December 23 to figure things out, that's when the rotation ended and med students went on Christmas break.

On the drive home I felt relieved. At least everything was out in the open, and my father was right; I needed to finish the rotation. It was the right thing to do. But looking back, I know that if I had walked away at that time, if I had made the decision to move on to something else, that my life wouldn't have been shaken up and turned upside down and inside out. Like Dad said, there's a reason for everything.

FIVE

We meet no ordinary people in our lives.

—C. S. Lewis

Meghan was up and out of bed before anyone else. She ran to the park and hovered around the massive oak tree, waiting. *She should be along soon,* Meghan thought. *Here she comes.* Meghan pretended to check her laces as the woman in the neon cap pushed a button on her stop-watch and took off. Meghan bolted upright and ran after her. The young woman's legs were longer than Meghan's, and her strides were fluid and graceful. But Meghan pushed hard, her pace gradually quickening.

The woman slowed to a jog and began walking up the hill on her way out of the park. Meghan shook out her arms and legs and walked along the lake before she finally fell to the ground, and rolled around in the grass, laughing. *I did it. I finally did it.*

. . .

Charlie snapped the television off when Meghan walked into the room dressed like a burly football player. It was the Halloween party at the hospital, and she was going to push Charlie in the parade of costumes. Charlie got down to business right away. "Did you run this morning?" Meghan nodded. "Was she there?" Meghan nodded again. "Did you beat her?" Meghan lowered her head. "Oh come on," Charlie said, disappointed. "You gotta beat her someday."

Meghan raised her head and smiled. "I did."

Charlie let out a whoop and pumped his arm in the air, as though Meghan had just scored a winning run. "I knew it'd happen someday. Next stop: the Olympics."

"How about, next stop: Halloween Party? Come on; get your costume on. Besides, I can't train for the Olympics while you're in this hospital bed. If you're going to coach me, you've got to be out in the field with me."

"I'm getting out of here just as fast as I can," he said, cracking his knuckles.

"Stop doing that," she said, leaving Leslie to help him with his costume. "Or you're going to have ape hands like all those wrestling freaks."

Meghan's family arrived early to help with the party; Luke was dressed like a fireman, and Olivia ran around the unit wearing red tights and leotard and a black hat with a piece of white rope bobbing from the top. Meghan found a wheelchair and pushed it back to Charlie's room, where she found him dressed as Charlie Chaplin, waiting for her. Leslie stood nearby, smiling, proud of her creation.

Leslie helped Charlie into the wheelchair, and Meghan pushed him to the pediatric unit, through the parade of costumes that filled the hallway. The staff clapped and cheered as the children, dressed like Disney characters, horror monsters, and superheroes, filed by. Med students had been volunteered to man the empty patient rooms as the children went from door to door yelling, "Trick or treat."

I was standing behind a door when I heard a loud knock. I opened it to find a small boy dressed as a fireman and a little girl with a rope sticking out of her hat. I tried to make out her costume.

"What are you today?"

"A firecracker," she said, beaming. Her mother sighed and nodded.

"I always thought firecrackers were loud and annoying, but now I know different because you're quiet and very pretty." She opened her mouth, embarrassed, and hugged her mother's waist. "What's your name?"

"Olivia." I put candy in her bag.

"Olivia sounds like the name of a princess. Are you a princess?"

Olivia shook her head and buried her face in her

mother's side. Her mother thanked me for the candy and pulled her daughter toward the next room. Olivia peeked up at me, smiling. "Hey, what's your name?" she yelled from down the hall.

"Nathan."

" 'Bye, Nathan," she said, reeling from her first crush.

How could I have known then that that little girl would remember my name? That simple act would confirm again that sometimes God uses the smallest of messengers to help get our attention.

The next morning I pulled a hooded sweatshirt over my head and slipped on a pair of sweatpants. I called William and asked if he wanted to go for a run. He didn't. William hated to run. I persisted, and he walked into my apartment wearing a pair of orange shorts over his sweatpants. I looked at him, wondering if it was a joke or not.

"What?" he asked. "Don't runners always wear shorts over their jogging pants?"

"I don't think so."

He looked down at himself. "I swear I saw this in a magazine on some big-name runner. Name some big-name runners, and I'll tell you if it was that guy or not."

I laughed and grabbed my keys. "No big-name runner would wear an outfit that looked like that."

William checked himself out before following me out the door. "Am I still like Shaft," he yelled down at me on the stairs.

"Even Shaft couldn't be cool in that outfit," I said, sliding behind the wheel of the truck.

We drove to the park and started our run. "Hold on, man," William said, pulling me back. "Don't go so fast. What's the point of running, anyway?" I looked at him and shook my head. He crouched to the ground and untied his shoe. "I need to fix my shoe. You go ahead and I'll catch up." I left him there, knowing William's run was over for the day.

I ran a few laps around the lake. I pushed myself hard until the sweat rolled down my back. Running had always been a good stress reliever for me, although recently it seemed as if nothing was relieving the stress anymore. I ran faster, wondering why I couldn't be more like my father. I'd been asking myself the same question ever since I was a child.

I remember writing a letter to my mom. I must have been about ten at the time:

Dear Mom,

When I grow up I hope I can be like Dad and even work in the garage with him. Sometimes he lets me play with the jacks and the lifts and I'm really good with them.

I love you,
Nathan

I laughed at the thought. Working in a garage would have been so much easier than going into medicine. People always said that I was like my father because I was quiet, but Dad's qualities ran much deeper than his silence.

Many times, I'd awaken in the night and see light coming from the living room. I'd creep there and find my father sitting alone, flipping through the family album, looking at pictures of my mother. From time to time, he would lean his head back against the sofa, his eyes closed. Watching him, I always imagined that he was entering a secret passageway, one that brought the moments captured in those pictures to life—those times with Mom that were so sweet, yet so painful to think about. Sometimes, I would tiptoe into the room and sit next to him on the sofa, but usually I would just go back to my bed without letting him know I was there. Somehow, even as a small boy, I recognized that those moments were sacred for him, special times he had carved out to be alone with my mother.

"God didn't take your mother," he'd always tell me, echoing what Mom had told me weeks before her death. "He received her. There's a difference." He had promised my mother that he would explain that to me until I finally understood.

One Saturday, Dad was working on Lorraine's car in our driveway when she made a comment about how God had taken my mother to Heaven. "He didn't take

her," I said, protesting. "He received her." My father slid out from underneath the car and looked at me. On that day, he realized that I understood. And he was right. I knew that God wasn't striking people with disease; I knew He was loving. My mother had shown me that love before she died. And after her death, though my father wasn't as comfortable with words as she had been, he gave that love hands and feet and wings every day; but I never understood why she *had* to die.

"God loved your mother very much," he'd tell me, trying to comfort me after I'd awoken from a nightmare and gone into his room. As a boy, I had a recurring dream that he'd died, too. "He loved her so much that he stopped the pain she was in," my father explained. He'd lift the covers on his bed and let me crawl in next to him. "Go back to sleep," he'd say, kissing my head. I'd try, but often I'd lie awake, thinking about my mother: *If God knew she was going to be sick, why didn't He make her better? Why pray at all if people are just going to die anyway? Why do so many good people have to die?* And as many times as I'd ask those questions, I never found any answers. All I knew was that I would never be as strong as my father.

William stepped onto the path and broke my concentration. "Unless somebody's chasing you, there's no reason to run that fast," he said, stretching.

"Are you ready to break a sweat?" I asked.

"As long as it doesn't drip down into my shoes."

A female runner slowed down to pass us, turning back

to look at me. She stopped and walked up to us. "Is this official doctor stuff?" she said. I looked at her, and she smiled the prettiest smile I've ever seen. "We met a few days ago when you were walking in the clearly designated running side of the hallway." I remembered who she was; I just wasn't used to women coming up and starting a conversation with me. William picked up his legs and ran in place.

"I gotta keep moving," he said. "I'm losing my stride." He leaned toward me, and whispered, "Keep it together this time." William knew I was notorious for blowing it with women. It wasn't in my genes to be suave and cool. I watched him run off and nearly laughed. For somebody who was so agile on the basketball court, William was a lousy runner. I walked with my new friend around the lake.

"I'm Meghan Sullivan, by the way," she said, extending her hand.

"Nathan," I said.

Megan noticed William, who was no longer running but talking with two women on the other side of the lake. He met women everywhere he went, and they always loved him. "I think your friend has lost his stride," she said, watching William.

"No, I think he's definitely found it." She laughed, and I noticed how pretty she was, even early in the morning, without makeup. I put my hands in my pockets and

thought about her name; it was so familiar. "Are you the Sullivan who's organizing the scholarship run at the hospital?" She turned toward me and her eyes lit up.

"Did you hear about it?"

"I signed up as a sponsor." I looked at her, remembering something. "Denise said you're one of the fastest runners in the state." She was embarrassed and didn't say anything. "She also said you were one of the heart patients."

"I like to think of myself as a close, personal friend of Dr. Goetz, not as a heart patient."

I smiled, wondering why anyone would want to be friends with Dr. Goetz. "Why are you such close friends with him?" I said, playing along.

"A ventricular septal defect that never closed." Hole in the heart. I looked at her, and she read my mind. "I don't know why I can run. Ever since I was a little girl, doctors said I'd live a normal life, but I'd just never be able to overexert myself."

"Doesn't running qualify as 'overexerting' yourself?" I asked, knowing the answer.

"Yes. Dr. Goetz said running would be out of the question."

"How about a dart? Would they have let you dart somewhere?" She grinned and suppressed a laugh.

"If it was a slow dart."

"Same with a dash?"

"A slow dash would be fine, but I could never make a mad dash anywhere." I laughed out loud, and Meghan joined me. She was attractive, athletic, *and* funny.

"Have you ever been concerned when you run?" I asked. She shook her head.

"My mind knows there's something wrong with my heart—I've seen the X rays; I know it's defective. But when I run, it's like my heart doesn't know it. It's as if I was created to do it. Do you know what I mean?"

"Yes," I said, unsure whether I believed that or not, because I couldn't imagine what I was created to do.

"If something happened, it'd just be part of the race. Like your job. You have great days when people are healed, but there are days when they're not, where nothing you do will make them better. You take the bad with the good but in the end, the good will always outweigh the bad." Again, I wasn't sure if I believed that or not. "What kind of doctor are you?" she asked.

"I'm not a doctor. I'm a third-year med student."

"Are you studying to be a cardiologist?" I told her I wasn't. "Why not? The heart's where all the action is. Without the heart nothing happens."

"That's exactly what they teach us in med school. They say, 'without the heart, everything goes splat.' " I made a nice wet sound for dramatic effect, and she laughed. I was on a roll.

"So what's it like being a med student?"

"Oh, it's as many cups of weak coffee you can stomach a day and so much more."

"So what you're saying is that with the urine samples, catheters, bedpans, and weak coffee . . . it's all glamour, right?"

"And all of it could be yours if you want to go to school for the rest of your life." Meghan was easy to talk to; for once I wasn't stumbling over my tongue. "What year are you?" I assumed she must be in her fourth year of college.

"I'm a freshman." I snapped my head and looked at her. I couldn't believe it. She seemed so much older than the other freshmen I knew from the university.

"I thought you were older," I said.

"I'm nineteen. I missed the cutoff day for kindergarten by one day." Still, I thought she was in her twenties.

"What are you studying?" I asked.

"Just the basics now because I'm not sure, but I think I'd like to teach."

"You want to be a gym teacher?" She bent over, laughing. "What? Is that not politically correct? Is it a recess facilitator?"

"People haven't called them gym teachers in years. I should have known it'd be some guy trapped inside a hospital drinking weak coffee."

"Now you see what all my loans are paying for."

"I want to teach high school and coach. Maybe teach social studies and health—" I stopped her there.

"I had health in eighth grade. Our textbook was called *Healthy Living and You*." She looked at me and stared. I held up my hands. "I'm telling you the truth . . . as best I can remember it. Mrs. Pringle taught the class and she stood about five-foot-five and weighed 180 on a thin day." Meghan put her face in her hands and shook her head back and forth. "We were taught healthy living by a woman named after a potato chip and shaped like a cookie."

"That was not her name!"

I held up a hand and crossed my heart with the other.

"I swear it was. And her husband's name was Lemmy. Lemmy Pringle. Do you think he got beat up as a kid?"

"Maybe Pringles' chips weren't around when he was a kid."

"It wouldn't matter. With a name like that you were just begging bullies for a beating." We both laughed, and I found myself not wanting the conversation to end. William bounded back down the hill toward me. I shook my head at the sight. I couldn't understand how someone dressed like that could attract not just one, but two women so early in the morning.

"I've got to get to the hospital," he said, breathing hard as if he'd been exercising all morning.

"Headed back into the world of glamour?" Meghan asked. I nodded and walked toward William.

"Yep. I hope we run into each other again, Miss Pringle." I walked up the hill and could hear her laughing. I couldn't remember having a better day at the park.

That afternoon Meghan stretched alongside her teammates on the track. Every day, she looked forward to practice, first because she loved it, but also because she loved her coach, Michele Norris. Michele had a way of coaching that brought the best out in her. Michele was thirtysomething and single, and the team loved teasing her about dating. It seemed they were always trying to set her up with an eligible uncle, cousin, brother, or even handyman. Michele knelt beside Meghan on the track. "Has Charlie told you to shave off another second?" she asked.

Meghan pulled her foot toward her, stretching her upper thigh. "No."

"What?" Michele said, feigning disbelief. "We've got a big meet here. He should have been demanding things days ago!" She gave Meghan's arm a playful squeeze and rallied her runners, instructing them to run warm-up laps for the day's meet.

When Meghan stood up, it felt as though her legs would buckle. She had been dragging ever since her morning run in the park, which was odd, because the run usually left her energized. She shook out her legs and rolled her neck from side to side. Once Meghan started

running, the laps came easier. Running always made her feel better.

Meghan paced back and forth on the field, waiting for her race to be called. She looked up into the stands and waved at her family. Luke and Olivia were already on their feet waving with both hands.

Coach Norris put her hand on Meghan's back. "Ready?" Meghan nodded, keeping her head down. "Run it like you did on Friday and you'll pin another ribbon on Charlie." When her race was called, Meghan blended in with all of the other runners standing thirty-to-forty deep at the line, but when the gun fired she bolted to the front position. Jim Sullivan jumped to his feet, cheering her on. Luke and Olivia screamed, "Go, go, go, go," in rapid-fire succession. They watched her wend her way through the woods and disappear.

"Ten minutes in," Jim said, staring at his watch. "Ten-and-a-half minutes in," he said, thirty seconds later. "Eleven-oh-two now. Eleven-ten."

"Would you stop that babbling, Jim?" Allison said. "You're making me a nervous wreck over here." Jim tried to be more discreet but couldn't keep his eyes off the second hand.

"Eleven-forty-five," he said, whispering into Luke's ear. Allison shook her head. This was why she never watched sports with him at home; her nerves were always frazzled by the time the event was over. Jim spotted a head or two at the end of the meadow. He stood to

his feet and scanned the figures looking for Meghan—*here she comes*—and then he looked down at his watch. "Thirteen minutes," he said, excited.

"She's running faster than Friday, Allison." He realized what he was doing and sat down in silence. Allison stood and watched Meghan run toward the finish line, now glancing at Jim for an update, but he remained quiet.

"Well, come on, Jim! What's her time?" Allison shouted. Jim jumped to his feet and held his arm up so that Allison could see his watch.

"Thirteen-forty," he said, his excitement building. "She's never run this fast!" The stands began to shake as people realized what was happening. Cheers erupted for Meghan as she stretched across the finish line in first place.

"Fifteen-twenty!" Jim yelled, loud enough for everyone around him to hear. Allison shushed him, embarrassed that she was the only member of her family with any civility. Meghan walked to the side of the track and bent over, trying to catch her breath. Allison stood taller to get a better look. *Stand up, baby,* she thought. *Straighten up.* Meghan shook it off, straightened up, and walked toward Coach Norris. "That's the way to run a race!" Michele said, hugging her tight.

"Charlie better be happy with my time," Meghan said, gasping. She was walking with Coach Norris toward the rest of the team when she collapsed.

• • •

"I'm fine," Meghan said for the hundredth time. Dr. Goetz stuck a thermometer in her mouth and listened to her heart.

"Any chest pain or breathing problems?" She shook her head. "At your checkup six months ago you were nauseous and achy. Any of that now?"

"Just a little tired and my muscles hurt," she said, balancing the thermometer in her mouth. "I've had a headache, but it's no big deal."

Dr. Goetz took the thermometer out of her mouth, looking at it. "No fever," he said. He washed his hands and leaned against the sink, drying them. "If you had a fever, it would have made sense as to why you collapsed. Since there is no fever, I'm concerned you might have an arrhythmia." Meghan sighed. She was familiar with the term; it was an abnormal heartbeat pattern. "That would decrease how well your heart performs, causing you to faint."

"If I had an arrhythmia, I wouldn't have been able to race today," Meghan said.

"I'd like to put you on telemetry overnight so I can monitor the heart for any irregularities."

"Overnight," Meghan said, frustrated. "Why?"

"Well, given your history and the fact that you're my favorite girl, I'd feel a whole lot better if you were here so we could enjoy your company."

"What's telemetry?" Allison asked.

"We'll put several patches on her chest with wires—kind of like an EKG—and we'll be able to monitor the heartbeat day and night at a workstation where computers will warn us of any problems. I also want to do some blood work to rule out anything else," Dr. Goetz said.

Meghan groaned and flopped back on the examining table. "Not more blood! Every time I come here you people squeeze me for more blood."

When the X rays came back Dr. Goetz walked to Meghan's room and sat down. "No physical change in the heart," he said, holding the X rays to the light. "But we'll still keep you overnight to make sure there's no change in the heart pattern." Meghan shook her head; she was not happy.

"If I have to stay here, can I at least be in Charlie's room?"

"In pediatrics?" Dr. Goetz asked.

"If it's just one night, who cares," Meghan said. Dr. Goetz threw his arms up in the air, surrendering.

"All right! I'll do anything to get on your good side again." He walked into the hall, and Jim and Allison followed. "I honestly suspect she'll go home tomorrow," he said.

"I was so afraid it was going to be something serious," Jim said.

Dr. Goetz smiled. That's exactly what he'd been afraid of, too.

. . .

When I got to the hospital that afternoon I went to the lounge to hang my coat in my locker. It was jammed. I was used to this. While I jiggled the handle I banged on the bottom left side. It opened every time. A nurse stopped me on my way out. "Claudia in pediatrics has been buzzing for you." I walked back into the lounge and picked up the phone.

"You've got a little girlfriend up here in 1216 who's been asking about you," Claudia said. Besides Charlie, I didn't know any of the other patients in that unit.

"Who is it?"

"Obviously an admirer of yours. She's been asking about you since she got here an hour ago. If you have the time, you might want to swing by and say hello." I hung up the phone, grabbed a soda, and drank it on my way to pediatrics. I walked toward 1216 and recognized it as Charlie's room, but I knew he didn't have a sister. I stood outside the door and listened to the chatter of little voices.

"What's your favorite word," a small voice asked.

"Love," a woman said.

"What's your least favorite word?"

"Yuck." The little voice laughed.

"I always say yuck, Mommy."

"I know."

I peeked my head inside the room and saw Charlie and his mother and another woman I didn't know. "You came," the owner of the voice I'd been listening to shrieked, making me turn on my heels. It was Olivia.

"Well, of course I would come see Olivia." She was surprised I had remembered her name, and her mouth dropped open; she covered it with both hands. She pointed a small finger in my face.

"What's your favorite word?"

"Rhinoceros. I like how it rolls off the tongue." She giggled and shook her head.

"What's your least favorite word?"

"Egg," I said with a straight face. "Listen how ugly that sounds . . . egg. Blah. What an awful word, and when some people mispronounce it and say 'aygg,' it sounds even worse." Everyone laughed at my odd choice of words. "Is it your birthday, Charlie?"

"No. They're all with Meghan." I spun to look, and saw Meghan sitting on the bed, wearing a hospital gown. I was shocked.

"What's going on? What happened?" I attempted to read Meghan's chart, but Olivia was separating the fingers on my hand, swinging it from side to side.

"I'm actually in here because I *don't* have a fever, if you can believe that. Dr. Goetz is blowing it out of proportion and making me stay overnight in the hospital!" Olivia let go of my hand, and I was able to scan Meghan's chart. Dr. Goetz was observing her for a possible heart arrhythmia. "I'm being held against my will," Meghan said, watching my face.

"You collapsed?" I asked. She shrugged it off.

"I've been tired, that's all. I'll guarantee you I don't have what Dr. Goetz is checking me for."

"It's good that he's keeping you," I said. She rolled her eyes.

"You medical people are always so serious."

My beeper sounded, and I pressed the button to turn it off. There is a brief time in a med student's life when he feels important to have a beeper; but months into wearing it, he begins to dread the sound. I wanted to stay longer and talk with Meghan about what happened, but I couldn't. I walked toward the door.

"Will you come back later?" Charlie asked.

"Please," Olivia begged, holding my hand.

"Please," Meghan said, smiling. I walked out the door, realizing that smile was going to occupy my mind for the rest of the day.

Early in the evening I remembered I had promised Olivia I'd come back to see her, which meant I'd also see Meghan again. I stuck my head inside the door but could see that Charlie was sleeping. Meghan saw me and propped herself up, smiling. I pulled the divider curtain to keep the noise down for Charlie.

"So where is everybody?"

"They'll be back soon, but Olivia said she was going to die if she didn't eat. She's the drama queen of the fam-

ily." She motioned for me to sit. "Could you stay till everybody gets back?" I looked at my watch to see what time it was and discovered it had stopped again. I shook my wrist and tapped the face till the second hand moved. I knew my pager would beep soon enough, but in the meantime I was more than happy to stay with Meghan.

"How are you feeling now?"

"I'm fine," she said. "I've been fine since I got here. Honestly, there's nothing wrong."

"Maybe so, but it's still good that Dr. Goetz . . ." She held up her hand, stopping me.

"I'm going to scream if one more of you people in white tells me that it's good that Dr. Goetz kept me overnight." I smiled and kept quiet.

"Meghan Sullivan sounds like a nice Irish name," I said, changing the subject.

"It used to be O'Sullivan, but a hundred years ago it wasn't good to be different, so they dropped the O. Of course there was barely any Irish left by the time my dad was born. We're mostly a Heinz 57 bunch now."

"None of the pure Irish left?"

"My great-grandfather was the last of the full breeds. He died before my father was born—cirrhosis of the liver. Same with my grandpa—he died before I was born of alcohol poisoning. My dad dried out before he married my mom. He always says that alcohol took him down, but a little five-foot-four-inch woman picked him up. He's helped out at AA for years."

⁂

Meghan and I talked about music—she loved Ella Fitzgerald. "What about all the hip acts that college kids love? Do you like any of them?"

"Like who?"

"I don't know all their names. Snoop Diggity Do and all those hip cats." Meghan shook her head and laughed. We talked about movies—she loved anything made before 1964. No wonder I thought she was older; she was an old soul in a young body.

"So what's your favorite movie?" I asked.

"*To Kill a Mockingbird.*" My mother would have liked Meghan. She made my father and me watch *To Kill a Mockingbird* with her when I was in first grade. It must have been the twentieth time she'd seen it, but she still cried at the parts that made her weepy-eyed the first nineteen times.

"Does your family live here?" she asked.

"They're about an hour away. Well, my dad and grandmother are. My sister's in college."

"And your mom?" Meghan said, sitting up in the bed.

"She died when I was eight."

"Of what?"

"Cancer."

"So that's why you want to be a doctor."

"I think that's how it started."

"So I bet you're studying oncology." I smiled and she looked me over. "You don't look like an oncologist to me." I looked down at myself.

✯

"What do I look like?"

"You remind me of Dr. Goetz." A gust of air rushed through my mouth, and I grabbed my head. "You do!" In my mind it wasn't a compliment to be compared with Dr. Goetz. "You must be studying pediatrics or something with kids, right?" I groaned inside, but knew I should just tell her the truth and be done with it.

"I'm actually finishing up this rotation and getting out of medical school."

"Why would you do that when you're so good at it?" I shook my head and smiled.

"I just don't think it's right for me."

"Well, I do," she said, surprising me. "Trust me, I know how doctors are around kids, and you're amazing. You've got my little sister right here." She held her pinky in my face. "Maybe it's not right for you now, but what about all those patients who are going to need a doctor like you? You need to finish up for them." She smiled and folded her hands. "I'm going to get off my soapbox now."

"Phew," I said, pretending to wipe sweat from my forehead.

"So what about you?" I asked. "What about all these scholarships people are buzzing about?" She smirked as if what she did wasn't all that remarkable. "So, what makes you so good?"

"I found someone to pace myself with," she said, sharing her secret. "You always have to run with someone better than you." For a brief moment I felt ashamed.

I had been pacing myself with Dr. Goetz, someone better than me, someone who could have made me better at what I do, but instead of choosing to run alongside him, I chose to take the easy way out and run away. In annoyance I tapped my watch again. "What's wrong with your watch?"

"It stops every now and then. All I have to do is tap it or snap the back where the battery is and it starts working again."

"Why don't you get a new one?"

"My mother wanted me to have this one. It works okay, I just need to coax it along every once in a while." Meghan watched me flip the watch over and thump the back of it.

"The watch isn't your mother, you know. It's just a reminder." Dr. Goetz entered the room, and I stood to leave.

"Are you moving in on another one of my best girls?" I backed away toward the door.

"Hey, I don't want no trouble. I didn't know she was your girl."

"Oh please," Meghan said. I smiled at her, anxious to leave the room now that Dr. Goetz had arrived. "Will you come by again?"

"There was a day when she used to ask me the same thing," Dr. Goetz said, lowering his head. I left the room, smiling. It was going to be a good day at the hospital, after all.

. . .

I couldn't make it to Charlie and Meghan's room until later in the evening. I wasn't sure if either one of them would be awake, but wanted to say good night if they were. I stuck my head inside, but both of them looked asleep. I started to close the door when I heard crying inside the room. I followed the sound to Meghan's bedside and sat down. "Are you in pain?" I said, whispering. She wiped her eyes and shook her head back and forth on the pillow. "What's wrong?"

"I'm just feeling sorry for myself." I sat down and she looked at me. "No offense, but I'm really sick of hospitals."

"I guess that's why it never makes any of the favorite vacation destination lists." She tried to smile, but wasn't in the mood. "You'll be out of here tomorrow."

"Tomorrow's too late." She was frustrated.

"For what?"

"There's an all-night charity dance at the university, and all my friends are there. Not that I'm some great dancer, but I'd rather be there than in here." I handed her a tissue and headed for the door.

I ran to the nurses' station and grabbed the boom box and set it on a table in the waiting room. I whispered my plan to the nurses, and one of them disconnected the wires from Meghan's chest. I pushed a wheelchair to Meghan's side. The nurse winked at me as she left the room; she would keep this a secret.

“What’s that?” Meghan asked, looking at the wheelchair.

“What does it look like? It’s a limo.” I slipped a lab coat over her arms. “And this is the finest Italian silk dress that I could find in the storage closet.” She smiled and sat in the chair. I grabbed her Ella Fitzgerald CD out of the portable CD player by her bedside and wheeled her to the waiting room, where I had moved all the chairs up against the wall. The nurses watched from the desk as I popped the CD into the boom box and pushed play. I offered her my hand. “Could I have this dance?” She was embarrassed but offered me her hand. I danced her around the room, dipping and spinning her till laughter replaced the tears. She twirled under my arm, and the nurses behind the desk laughed, watching us. At the end of “Mack the Knife” I dipped her so far that she reached back and touched the floor for dramatic effect.

In one of the letters she wrote during her last week, my mother said:

Dear Nathan,

I know you think it’s gross now, but one day you’ll see a young girl and your heart will skip a beat when she smiles at you. That was how I felt about your father the first time I saw him. Then the moment will come when you know you love her and if it’s true love, the day will come when you realize that you can’t live without her. People may try to tell you that love doesn’t last these days but don’t believe them. Love can and still does last, and I know the love you’ll have will be the lasting kind.

I pulled Meghan up and she lost her footing. I held tighter to keep her from falling and looked in her eyes; at that moment my heart skipped a beat. She caught my gaze and grew still, looking at me. Embarrassed, she took her hands from my shoulders. I pushed the wheelchair toward her and knelt on one knee, placing each of her feet on a footrest. "Let's get you back to your room," I said. She sat down, looking up at me.

"Do I have to? Unless it's for medical reasons I'd like to stay here a while longer." I cleared my throat and sat down in one of the waiting room chairs.

"I don't think Dr. Goetz would have a problem with that." I fumbled for something to say.

"Olivia's never going to forgive me," she said. "I just danced with the man she loves." I smiled. "That was better than dancing with a bunch of college guys any day. Thank you."

"It was my pleasure." I smiled, and she looked at me. "Really." She looked down and fidgeted with the hospital gown on her lap. Now she was fumbling for something to say.

"You're a good doctor."

"I'm not a doctor," I said. "I told you, I'm barely a student anymore. How would you know anyway? I've never treated you."

"Because I've been around doctors all my life. I know the good ones from the bad ones. You're gifted at it." I shook my head. "You are! My dad says a gift is something

that comes so naturally that you don't even realize you're good at it until somebody points it out." I cocked my head, and she laughed. "It's true. You're a natural at this, but you don't know it." I didn't say anything. She sighed and gave up. "Will you run in the scholarship race?"

"I'll run it with bells on," I said, meaning it.

I looked down and tapped the face of my watch. Meghan shook her head. "Life's zooming past you while you stand around tapping that watch." I wheeled her back to the room and helped her into bed. "Thank you, Nathan." I smiled and turned to look at Charlie, but he was asleep, so I slipped out the door, nodding for the nurse to attach the wires again. I'd be leaving for home soon, and I knew that I'd think of Meghan for the rest of the night.

Charlie stirred shortly after midnight. Rich was lying on a cot, but he sat up when he heard Charlie move. He stood and walked to his side.

"You okay?" Rich asked.

Charlie nodded. "Just tired."

"You get some sleep and when you wake up, we'll be here waiting," Rich told his son.

"Dad, I'm tired, but I'm not sleepy," Charlie said. "Tell me about Alaska."

Rich's first year in the Air Force was spent in Alaska,

and Charlie loved to hear his dad talk of hiking through the mountains and seeing moose and caribou and bears and of fishing for halibut and watching sea otters or walrus play near the boat. "I'll take you someday," Rich said, "and we'll fish and hike and watch the beluga whales come in every day to eat."

Five years into his marriage to Leslie, Rich had left the Air Force. He later claimed that leaving was the worst decision he ever made. He went from one failed job interview to another as Charlie's medical bills mounted. "All I do is go to an interview, then go home and wait," he said time and again in frustration. "While I'm waiting someone else is getting my job!" Charlie knew his parents weren't getting along, and their arguments scared him.

"Daddy, tell me about Alaska," Charlie said to his father during a particularly heated battle. Maybe, Charlie hoped, he'd get his father's mind off of money and bills.

"Charlie, we're never going to Alaska. We'll never be able to afford it, so stop asking about it." Rich regretted the words the moment he said them. He wanted to tell Charlie that he would take him to Alaska, but he knew it would be a lie. There was no way they could afford it; they'd never be able to afford it. Leslie's part-time job wasn't enough to live on, and the stress of wondering how they would pay their bills each month only worsened.

When the bill collectors started sending notices in the mail, Rich spiraled deeper into depression. He left when Charlie was five and Matthew was three. "But we'll be all right," Leslie pleaded as he packed his bags. Rich didn't believe her. It seemed clear to him that it would be better for his boys if he left. He'd send whatever he could, still do whatever it took to support them, but he had to go. He wasn't the father or the husband his family needed.

Five months into the separation he called Leslie. "I need to come home." She listened. "It's better to be poor with you and the boys than to be crazy without you." Rich finally found a steady job driving a truck for the package delivery service. But they were told they'd have to wait to get into a house since Rich didn't show a solid income for over a year.

"I'm sick of waiting! I can't stand this apartment," Rich said. He and Leslie were sitting on their bed with Matthew between them. Charlie listened at the doorway. "We're decent people, Leslie. We work hard. That should count for something."

"I'll do it with you, Daddy." Charlie jumped up on the bed and edged between his parents, bouncing Matthew up and down on the mattress. His mom and dad had separated before; Charlie would do anything to prevent it from happening again.

"Do what?" his father asked.

"I'll wait with you. I'd wait forever if we have to."

When Charlie was a baby, Rich and Leslie waited in agony as doctors diagnosed his condition, then they suffered the agonizing wait as Charlie went from one surgery to another. He had been healthy, with few problems for the last several years. Five months ago, Dr. Goetz admitted him to the hospital for tests when it was apparent his heart was malfunctioning.

Dr. Goetz sat in a chair opposite the couple, leaning toward them. "Charlie's heart has developed an irregular beat."

Leslie held tight to Rich's hand. "What does that mean?" Rich asked.

"It might just mean that we need to put him on medications."

"Or," Leslie asked, knowing there was more.

"Or it could mean that his heart is weakening," Dr. Goetz said.

Tears streamed down Leslie's face. When Rich and Leslie were ready, Dr. Goetz led Charlie into the room and told him a portion, but not all of what he'd told his parents. Charlie looked at his mother and could tell that she'd been crying.

He looked up at Dr. Goetz. "Have you treated a bunch of patients who have the same thing I have?"

"A whole bunch."

Charlie looked up at his parents and back at Dr. Goetz. "What's the worst thing about the medications?"

"Waiting to see if they work," the doctor told him.

A broad smile crossed Charlie's face. "No problem! We're great waiters!"

Charlie had fallen asleep as Rich told him story after story of Alaska. He opened his eyes and saw Rich sitting at his side, reading. "Still waiting, Dad?" Charlie asked.

Rich looked up from his book and smiled. "I'd wait forever if I have to, Charlie."

As promised, Dr. Goetz released Meghan in the morning. "No arrhythmia," he said, examining her. "But I want you to go home and rest for a few days till these flulike symptoms you have work themselves out." Meghan opened her mouth to protest but Dr. Goetz grabbed each side of her face. "No running. None."

"For how long?"

"A week."

"What! I'm better. You said so yourself."

"No, I said you don't have an arrhythmia, but you still collapsed from something, so no running. I hope this is the last I see of both of you for a while."

"Am I getting out, too?" Charlie asked.

Dr. Goetz pointed to the door. "Get out! Leave! Begone." Charlie threw the blankets off and swung his feet to the floor. "It's a good thing I don't take your excitement to get away from me personally, Charlie." Leslie laughed and helped Charlie gather his clothes. Alli-

son wrapped the cord around Meghan's CD player and stuck it in a canvas bag.

Meghan hugged Dr. Goetz. "Don't take it personally, Dr. Goetz." He stood at the door to leave.

"I won't. But I will take it personally if I don't get a moonlight dance."

Meghan looked at him, shocked. "Who told you?"

Dr. Goetz smiled and slipped out the door. "I've got eyes and ears all over this place."

Meghan ran to the door and yelled down the hall toward him. "Big-mouth nurses."

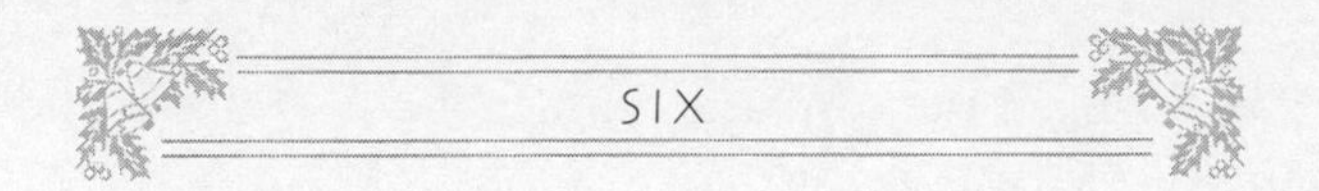

SIX

The supreme happiness in life is the conviction that we are loved.
—Victor Hugo

Early that morning, before most people had even eaten breakfast, I had already been vomited on in the ER. I changed into dry slacks (opting to throw away my soggy khakis) and made my way back to the ER for another full day of stress when I saw both Meghan and Charlie at the ER desk. Charlie saw me first. "We're getting out today," he said, excited to be going home. Meghan smiled.

"We wanted to let you know," she said. "I mean, we wanted to let you know that we wouldn't be upstairs in case . . ." She tried to find the right words. I let her squirm and smiled as she groped for a way to tell me she was leaving and that she'd like to see me again. "You know . . . in case anything medically comes up, and you need to reach us." Charlie gave her a confused look that nearly made me laugh. He had no idea what she was doing.

"Okay," I said. "If there are any charts or graphs or

X rays that I need to discuss with either one of you, I'll be sure to contact you at your respective homes." Charlie looked at me and scrunched up his face.

"I'm sure medical records has each of our home numbers," Meghan said, grinning. I watched as she walked with Charlie down the hall and realized I didn't care what happened for the rest of the day.

Meghan lay propped up on her living room sofa, resting. Two days of practice had come and gone, and she was unable to run in the meet scheduled for that night. She was getting restless. She hadn't gotten any more sponsors for the scholarship run, and that made her even more frustrated. "For the last time, you're not going," Allison said.

"Mom, it won't even take any energy. All I have to do is drive from place to place and ask people if they want to sponsor me in the run." Allison folded the basket of towels and shook her head.

"Dr. Goetz said rest, Meghan."

"I've missed two days of practice. All I've been doing is lying here. Who's going to sponsor a runner who doesn't run?"

Allison slipped into the kitchen and retrieved the phone book from a drawer. She picked up the telephone and plopped the phone and the book in Meghan's lap. "Let your fingers do the running for you."

Meghan stared at the phone book, then up at her mother. "You're no help at all." But she flipped to the yellow pages anyway and started with the A's. *Accountants and Attorneys*, she thought. *Maybe this won't be so hard*. She picked up the phone and made her first pitch.

"Hello, I'm organizing a scholarship run for heart patients. Would your company be interested in sponsoring me?" They weren't. Meghan hung up the phone, disappointed. *The least they could have done was listen to my pitch*. But come to think of it, she didn't have a pitch. She thought for a moment before dialing the next number. "Hello, I'm running to raise money for heart patients and am looking for people to sponsor me." The person on the other end of the line hurried her off the phone. Meghan hung up in frustration. This wasn't easy; it was annoying.

She made several more calls without sparking even a hint of interest. On her tenth try to an attorney's office, she got a nibble. "Layton and Associates," the woman said, answering the phone. "This is Jodie." Meghan threw her pitch again. Jodie Gavin had been working for Robert Layton for five years. She started in college, working afternoons and through summer vacations, before going full-time after graduation three years ago. Jodie never bothered Robert with unsolicited calls, but this one was different; the young woman on the other end of the line sounded so sincere. There was something in her voice that made Jodie want to help.

Meghan heard the phone click.

"Robert Layton," a man on the other end said. Meghan was startled at the sound of his voice. She'd never actually gotten past the secretary before. She stumbled as she made her appeal. "Who's running?" Robert asked. After so many rejections, Meghan hadn't expected questions.

"Uh, I am, and some of the staff and doctors from the hospital." Robert asked a few other questions, which, to Meghan's surprise, she answered with confidence. Her nerves were gone.

"Can you put me down for five hundred dollars?" Jodie smiled and closed Robert's door. Meghan's jaw dropped. She scribbled down Robert's information and gave him her name and phone number should he have any other questions. She hung up the phone and kicked the blanket off her legs. "Mom! You're never going to believe this!"

I called Meghan the next day and we made plans to get together Saturday after my rounds. When Saturday came I had no idea what Meghan and I would do that evening.

On my lunch break I decided to make a quick trip to Hope's room. When I saw her, I knew she wasn't herself that day: her face was drawn, and her upbeat disposition was gone. I sat down on the side of her bed and smiled. When she saw me a small tear ran down her cheek. She reached her arms for me, and I leaned down and hugged her.

“Is something wrong, Hope?” I whispered, wiping the tears from her face. “Do you need Dr. Goetz?”

She shook her head, resting it against my chest. “I’m sad, Dr. Andrews,” she said. I smiled; no matter what I did or said, nothing would convince Hope that I wasn’t a doctor. I pulled her from me so I could see her face.

“Why are you sad?”

“Because a little boy died for me.” A stream of tears covered her face, and I grabbed a tissue next to her bed. “A little kid died, and that makes me so sad.” I wiped her tears and hugged her again. “I can’t ever say thank you,” she managed to squeak between sobs.

“You say thank you every day,” I said, stroking the back of her hair. She looked up at me.

“How?”

“You open your eyes and you breathe.”

“But that’s not saying thank you,” she said.

“It’s the greatest thanks you could ever give, Hope, because every day when you open your eyes, it means you’re still here.”

“But I don’t know why I’m here and he isn’t.” I helped her lie back on her pillow and held on to her hand.

“He knows,” I said, patting her hand. “He knows everything now, and I just know that he’s so happy he could help you.” She was quiet for a moment.

“Are his mommy and daddy still sad?”

“Yes,” I said. “There will always be a part of them that will be sad because when someone we love dies, it’s like

a wound that will never fully heal. It gets better as time passes, but the wound just never heals up completely. Do you know what I mean?" Hope nodded, drawing a Pooh bear close to her. "But even though his parents are sad, they're so happy to know that there's a child somewhere in a hospital who is hugging a little Pooh bear today." Hope hugged Pooh tighter and kissed the end of his soft, black nose.

"How did they know to help me?" she whispered.

"Because they're people with a lot of love in their hearts. They didn't know who you were; they just knew that somewhere there was a child who was sick, and they wanted to help."

"Even though they were sad?"

"Right in the middle of their sadness, they knew that somebody needed help."

"And that was me."

"That was you," I said, pulling the sheets around her and Pooh. She motioned for me to come closer, as if she was going to tell me a secret. I leaned down and she wrapped her little arms around my neck, kissing my cheek.

"I love you, Dr. Andrews," she said, giggling. For a moment, I couldn't imagine the possibility of not working with children like Hope again. I patted her arm as her mother returned to the room, holding a cup of coffee and a stack of children's books and toys, anything she could find to help bring a smile to Hope's face. She saw that Hope was laughing again, and she looked at me, wondering what I had done to her child.

I wandered down to the cafeteria for a large cup of coffee and a sandwich for lunch, but maintenance had closed it off—a pipe had burst, flooding much of the kitchen floor. I walked across the street to Macbeth's, and for the first time ever I saw Dr. Goetz outside of the hospital. I didn't realize the chief of cardiology would set foot in a place like Macbeth's. I avoided eye contact, hoping he wouldn't see me, but I heard him say hello. I waved, acting as if I hadn't seen him there, and made my way to his table. "Have a seat," he said. I slid into a chair, uncomfortable to be sitting with him.

"How's the rotation going?" *He obviously hasn't heard*, I thought. I assumed that all the doctors knew which medical students were crashing and burning.

"I love meeting new patients," I said, avoiding the question.

"I can see that. Hope is impressed. That's not easy to do." I took a sip of coffee and shook my head.

"I don't know how you can keep yourself from not getting attached to kids like her and Charlie and Meghan."

"Who said I'm not attached?" He wiped his hands on a napkin. "I held Meghan when she was just a few days old. I can't tell you how old that makes me feel. Her par-

ents would take her to their family doctor, but they'd always bring her to me afterward, concerned about a diagnosis, or the use of certain medications. It got to the point where they were bringing her to me first whenever something was wrong." I couldn't imagine any other chief of cardiology seeing a patient on those terms.

"Why didn't you just tell them that you weren't their family physician?" He took the lid off a black coffee and swirled it round in the cup before taking a long drink.

"I don't know, but for whatever reason, when Meghan looked up at me with those huge blue eyes . . . I just knew that I needed to be her doctor. There's something about children who have a heart condition. They perceive life differently than the rest of us. They listen with the heart. They see things through the eyes of the heart. When a child sits in my office and looks at me, I know he or she sees right past the degrees and awards on the wall. They see *me*, and that's a terrifying thought." I never knew Dr. Goetz had a sense of humor.

"Do you remember all your patients from over the years?"

"I don't think I could place all the adults, but I remember the children." He was quiet. "I remember all of them." I knew he was talking about the ones he couldn't help. "I can see the picture of so many children in my mind, but they all have a big question mark stamped on them. Why did that child have heart disease? Why didn't he have a strong heart like other children? I lost a four-year-old two weeks after a transplant last year and her face will pop into my mind and I just can't explain why she's not running across a playground today." For the first time since I met him I realized that I liked Dr. Goetz. He didn't think he was superior in any way; he was more in touch with the fact that he was human than I was at the time.

"Did you ever want out?"

He leaned back and smiled. "I got out."

"When?"

"Eighteen years ago. I was out for six years." I couldn't believe that Dr. Crawford Goetz would ever walk away from medicine—from day one I just knew he had to have been a gunner in med school.

"Why did you leave?"

"I couldn't take the sadness anymore. Couldn't deal with the sickness. I was going home to my family depressed every day. I had taken my limit of people dying, so I took a job in landscaping. It had nothing to do with medicine. I could go out each day and break my back but never worry about another patient dying under my care."

"What brought you back?"

"The very thing that drove me away."

I don't know if Dr. Goetz said the things he did because he knew I was leaving med school or if he was just showing a student that even doctors walk through dark days, sometimes walking through years of darkness before finding their way back.

I left the restaurant and walked back to the hospital, thinking about my conversation with Dr. Goetz and about Hope and Charlie and so many of the kids in the pediatric unit. How could I live my life running from what scared me, when children were facing their fears head-on every day? I decided to take the coward's way out and think about that tomorrow.

I left the hospital at five that afternoon. I was picking Meghan up at six. I called earlier in the day to make sure she was feeling up to it, and she assured me she was, saying she was tired of resting when there was no reason to rest in the first place.

"When's the last time you went out on a date?" William asked, amused.

"I don't remember. All I know is none of the last ones went all that well, so I don't want to do what I did with them."

"What'd you do with them?"

"I took the last two girls to a museum."

William looked at me and shook his head. "You mean fossils?"

"I don't remember."

"Take her someplace nice to eat and try to charm her,"

he said, entering a patient's room. Then he stuck his head out the door. "If you can do that without fossils," he yelled after me.

I drove home, wondering how I would charm Meghan. I wasn't very good in that department, not at all like William. A thought occurred to me, and I opened the phone book. I had heard about a small theater in the next town over that played independent and classic films. I called them, and they were showing *The Philadelphia Story* with Katharine Hepburn. Perfect.

Olivia opened the door and smiled. "Are you and Meghan going out?" she asked. I nodded. Meghan put her hands on Olivia's shoulders, pulling her away from the door. To this day, I remember what Meghan was wearing that night: jeans and a dark brown pullover cable-knit sweater that looked stunning on her. Olivia dragged her father to the door.

"So you're the man who's stolen my little girl's heart," he said, swaying Olivia back and forth on top of his feet.

"Daddy, don't embarrass me," Olivia said.

"You can expect something a hundred times worse than this about ten years from now," Jim said. I liked Jim Sullivan. He reminded me of my father: No one was getting to his daughters without going through him first. I talked with him and Allison for a few minutes, long enough for them to discover my age, family background, future plans, and social security number, before I helped Meghan into my truck.

"Sorry about that," she said, as I climbed in. "It's easier to break into the Pentagon than it is to date one of Jim Sullivan's daughters."

I wanted to take Meghan to the Italian restaurant in town, one that made each course a meal in itself, but she wasn't interested.

"Oh, why don't we go to Macbeth's or some place where it's not so stuffy?" I knew then that my grandmother would love Meghan. I drove to Chuck's. "What's this?" Meghan asked.

"This is the best cheeseburger and shake in America," I said, pointing to the half-blown neon sign above the entrance. Meghan read the sign and laughed: THE BEST CHEESEBURGER AND SHAKE IN AMERICA.

I can't remember all we talked about that night. All I know is that it was effortless with Meghan. She was lovely and bright, and I couldn't help but think she was perfect . . . for me.

Dear Nathan,

You won't find a perfect person to love, so please don't think you will. But you will find someone who is perfect for you. She won't be everything you ever dreamed of. She will be more. So give her only your best—your heart, and all the love in the world!

Mom

I refrained from holding Meghan's hand during the movie. I didn't even put my arm around her; it was, after

all, our first date, and I've always been chicken, to say the least, so the decision not to do anything was easy for me. The temperature had dropped from the time I had picked Meghan up, colder than most Novembers in recent years, so after the movie I wrapped my jacket around her and helped her to the truck. I drove her home and scurried her to the front door, lowering my head to avoid the high wind. She got her key out and turned to look at me, shivering. "Keep my jacket," I said. "I'll get it some other time." I didn't know what to do, so I smiled and turned to leave. "I'll call you," I said.

"You can kiss me if you want." I turned back around, put my hands under my arms and looked at her. "I mean, it's okay, if that's what you were thinking. But if it's not what you were thinking, then I've just really embarrassed myself and . . ."

I grabbed her and kissed her and forgot about the cold and the wind and the fact that I had to get up at five o'clock in the morning.

Days later, I went to one of Meghan's cross-country meets and sat fourth bleacher up, by the "foghorn man," next to Olivia. Meghan looked up from the field and smiled at us. The air was crisp, and she was wearing spandex pants and a long-sleeved shirt with the university's name printed on the front. I zipped up my jacket and waited for her race to be called. Jim bolted out of his

seat the second the gun went off for Meghan's first race. He pumped his hand in the air, screaming, "*Go, baby; go, baby; go, baby,*" as Meghan blazed through the woods and across the countryside. Allison cowered in embarrassment, and I laughed. I had a feeling this was routine for them. Meghan was unbelievable; too fast for the competitors. She crossed the finish line in first place, and Jim pounded my back, shaking my shoulders.

I helped Meghan gather her things and walked her to my truck. We hadn't talked about her scholarship offers since her overnight stay in the hospital, but after I saw her run again I just had to bring it up. "When are you going to visit Stanford and Georgetown?" She sighed, leaning her head on the back of the seat.

"I have no idea. I don't know what to do anymore because I really love my coach here, I love the university." She grabbed my hand and smiled. "I love everything the city has to offer."

"But you can't stay here." She turned her head to look out the window. I pulled her shoulders around to face me. "When you run . . . it's one of the most unbelievable things I've ever seen. You're a star, Meghan. You were meant to shine. Those schools have the best running programs in the nation." She wasn't responding. "That has to be important for you. Running has got to be one of your dreams, right?"

"Sure, but I've got more dreams than that," she said.

"Like what?"

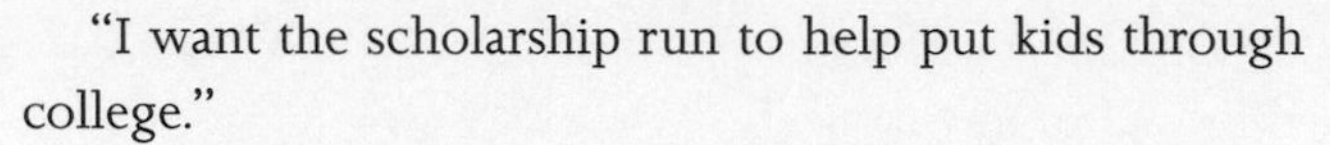

"I want the scholarship run to help put kids through college."

I nodded. "And you can work on that while you're at either school."

"I want to help change my small part of the world."

I nodded again and smiled. "You've already done that. What else?"

"I want to fall in love."

"I'm sure you will," I said. She looked at me and squeezed my hand.

"I'm sure I already have."

I should have told Meghan then and there that I loved her, but I didn't. I don't know why. I guess I just assumed there would be plenty of time left for me to do that.

Meghan and I were supposed to go out the next day, but she was tired and sore and had a headache that was keeping her in bed. I could tell by her voice that she didn't feel well.

"Whatever you do, don't tell Dr. Goetz," she said on the phone. "He'll throw me in a hospital bed and strap me down for a week." We rescheduled for the next day.

When I picked her up, she looked great. She didn't tell me that she felt lousy and that none of her symptoms had gone away.

I drove her out of the city and toward my hometown. I drove through town and up the road that led to the hill-

side where my grandparents once lived. I hadn't been on the road in years and had forgotten how windy it was. We made it to the top and I opened the door for Meghan. The November wind whipped through her hair, and she wrapped her coat around her; it was much colder on top. "What an incredible spot," she said.

I hadn't stood on top of this hill with another woman since my mother died. I watched as Meghan looked over the top of the ridge into the valley below. Her hair kept blowing in her eyes, and she tried in vain to keep it out of her face. She pulled it back and held it away with her hand; she had high cheekbones but the most delicate features. She was beautiful. The wind blew her coat open and she screamed, wrapping it around her again as she ran into me, burying her head in my chest. She wrapped her arms around me, and I smelled her perfume. Thanksgiving was just over three weeks away, then Christmas would be upon us before we knew it; and although I had no idea what I would do once my rotation was over, I knew that life didn't get much better than this.

SEVEN

The best and most beautiful things in the world cannot be seen or even touched. They must be felt with the heart.

—Helen Keller

Meghan grabbed two ibuprofen out of the bathroom cupboard and poured herself a glass of water in the kitchen. The two ibuprofen she'd taken earlier hadn't touched her headache, and she didn't want to be sick on Thanksgiving. She peeled potatoes and put them on the stove to boil. "Are these the last things that need to be done?"

"That's it," Allison said.

"Let me peel them," Michele said, sliding in next to Meghan at the sink.

"You're our guest today," Allison said. "You're not supposed to work." She opened a drawer and pulled out a tablecloth with fat turkeys all over it. "Here you go," she said to Michele. "If you want, you can set the table."

Meghan caught a glimpse of the tablecloth. "No, Mom. Please don't use that. The Pilgrims had better tablecloths than that thing."

Michele snapped the tablecloth in the air. "Do you normally line the turkeys up across like this?" Michele asked.

"Just make sure the fat one rests right in the center," Allison said, pulling the cloth over the table with the finesse of a fine artist.

Jim sliced the turkey and set it in the middle of the table. "I already know what I'm thankful for," Olivia said. Every year the Sullivans went around the table and said what they were thankful for, it was a tradition Allison started when Meghan was a baby. Jim set a thick slice of breast meat on Olivia's plate.

"All right," he said. "Olivia's going to start us off this year."

"I'm thankful for this," she said, pointing to the turkey on her plate. Luke was thankful for the snow that would soon be on its way, which meant early school dismissals. Allison's eyes misted over when she said she was thankful that her husband and her children were all in good health.

"Mom, you cry every year," Luke said, embarrassed.

"What are you thankful for, Daddy?" Olivia asked.

"That you're all right here at this table," Jim said.

They turned to look at Michele, who was busy filling her plate. She set her napkin in her lap and realized that everyone was looking at her. "You don't have to participate," Jim said, giving her an out.

"That's okay. I know exactly what I'm grateful for. My

father said there wouldn't be any money in teaching, that the hours would be long, and in the end I wouldn't be fulfilled. Well, the way I see it, one out of three isn't bad! My job is fulfilling. I love to teach, I love to coach, and I love the girls. And as an extra bonus I get to meet great people who open their homes to me on Thanksgiving."

Allison's eyes were tearing up again. "I bet your father is proud," she said, blowing her nose. "I bet he's so, so proud."

"All right, Meg," Jim said. "We're ready to eat. What are you grateful for this year?"

"What we have together," Meghan said. "Not everybody has what we have and we have it year-round, not just one day a year."

Allison's eyes were streaming by then. "For heaven's sake, Allison," Jim roared. "Go get a towel and mop yourself up so we can eat." Allison snorted through her nose and cried harder.

I picked Meghan up after my rounds ended. My grandmother had called me twice at the hospital to confirm that Meghan was still coming to Thanksgiving dinner. I opened the door to my father's house and Gramma and Rachel were practically sitting on the doorknob, waiting for us. I sighed and gave them a look, hoping they'd get the hint and back off. They didn't. I tried to lead Meghan into the house, but Gramma stopped her, taking her coat.

"My! What a pretty coat," she said. "Is that wool?" Meghan nodded. "I love wool. It's so warm, isn't it?" I smiled at Gramma's attempt at small talk. Rachel led Meghan to the sofa. I don't know why I'm always amazed at the information women are able to pump out of someone in five minutes or less, but watching the process in action always left me in awe. Meghan smiled, but never managed to get out much more than *uh-huh* or *hmm* during the grueling interrogation. It didn't matter though. Gramma had gathered enough information to base her opinion.

"She's so sweet," she whispered on her way into the kitchen.

Whatever nerves I had about Meghan meeting my family disappeared at the dinner table. In William's words, she was charming, and her laugh was infectious, even causing Dad to laugh out loud. She somehow managed to choke down her second Thanksgiving meal of the day, *mmming* and *ohhing* after each new thing she tasted.

When I stood to take Meghan home, Gramma jumped up and hugged her, asking her to come back soon. I walked Meghan to the front door of her house and noticed she looked tired.

"It's probably all the food I've eaten today," she said, laughing. "I'll sleep it off and feel great in the morning. You are coming over tomorrow, right?"

"Yes."

"And the next day?"

"Yes."

"And the day after that?" She smiled and my heart skipped a beat again. "Happy Thanksgiving," she said, leaning in to kiss me.

Happy Thanksgiving indeed!

I walked back into my father's house, and Gramma was asleep in her chair. Dad was still watching football. I noticed that Rachel wasn't in the room and assumed she was getting ready for bed.

"Meghan's nice," Dad said. I sat down on the sofa, watching the game. I always loved talking to my dad but when it came to talking about girls and dating, I just froze, not knowing what to say anymore. "What's her family like?"

"They're great," I said. "Really nice people." Dad looked over at me and knew I was squirming.

"She's really pretty," he said. I nodded. "Did you kiss her good night?"

"I'm trying to watch the game here, Dad," I said. He grinned, and I knew he was trying to get at me. He stood and grabbed his coat out of the closet. "Did you need something?" I asked. "I could have gotten it when I was out."

"I'll just be out for a while," he said, keeping his voice down.

"I can go get something for you, Dad."

"I'm just going out for coffee." Gramma snapped to attention in her chair. Dad's shoulders fell, and he rolled his eyes. She still had ears like a bat.

"Where are you having coffee?" she asked, curious.

"Over at Lydia's house," Dad said, pulling on his gloves before escaping out the door. Gramma threw her arms over her head and kicked her feet in the air, whooping in celebration.

"And it only took fifteen years!"

I went to find Rachel to tell her one of Gramma's ploys had finally worked. I saw her in Gramma's room, looking through the letters we had written to our mother.

I had always thought that Mom's death was gentler on Rachel than it was on the rest of us. She had no clear memories of Mom; all she had was what we told her along with the photo albums, the locket, and letters. I sat beside her on the floor and filed through the notes written with colorful markers, crayons, pencils, or ballpoint pens. Pictures of stick people or animals were often scribbled on the pages to help illustrate the letter.

I wrote this letter on what would have been Mom's thirty-fifth birthday:

Dear Mom,

It's your birthday today and I hope they made you the biggest cake in Heaven. We planted impatunce with Gramma. She said they were your favrite flour and that they'd be real real pretty in a few weeks. I hope you can see them.

I smiled, reading the rest of the poorly spelled letter. I scanned several letters, my memory blurred about many of them.

I wrote this one the Christmas after she died, when I was nine:

Dear Mom,

When I grow up I want to be a doctor so I can help peopel get better. I thought you'd want to know that on Christmas.

Merry Christmas! I still love you,

Nathan

Were it only that simple, I thought.

"I always wonder what she'd look like now, don't you?" Rachel asked. I nodded. Each year as I noticed gray hair in my father's head I wondered if Mom would be graying or if she'd still have the rich, dark color I always remembered. "I always wonder what we would do together now," Rachel continued. For the rest of our lives we would wonder about so many things.

I picked up a letter written in pencil when I was ten without the added touches of badly drawn dogs or ducks to jazz it up:

Dear Mom

Today Gramma explaned that you know why you died. She said God made sure bad things didn't happen to you. She said sumday I'll understud that better. I hope she's right.

I love you,
Nathan

When Rachel and I were still children I found a verse from the Bible written on a crumpled piece of paper at my father's bedside. "*. . . For I know the plans I have for you . . . plans to prosper you and not to harm you, plans to give you hope and a future.*" I studied the paper, but making no sense of it I took it to my grandmother. She read it and grew quiet.

"You need to put this back on your father's nightstand. These are words that are helping him." I took the paper from her and headed back to my father's bedroom. I stopped and turned to look at her.

"But I don't understand what they mean." She took my hand and led me into Dad's room, setting the paper back on the stack of books he kept on the table by his bed. She sat on the bed and stood me in front of her.

"Your father has obviously put this on top of his things so that he's reminded that there's a longer look of our life that we can't see. All we see is what's right in front of us." I looked down at the words again.

"I don't get it." She hugged me to her.

"I think that if your daddy didn't have a reason to hope, he'd have a hard time getting out of bed every day." I looked at her, confused. "He'll never understand why your mother had to leave us, none of us ever will; but she knows." I looked up at her. "As soon as she stepped into Heaven she could see the big picture of her life, and I bet when she saw it that her jaw dropped open and then I bet she started doing cartwheels and handstands and whatever else she used to do with you in the yard." I looked down at the words written in my father's handwriting on the paper.

"How does that help Dad?" She sighed and pulled me up on the bed beside her.

"Because if your daddy didn't believe it, he'd go absolutely crazy without your mother." I stared at the paper on the nightstand.

"My mother was a good person, wasn't she?"

"She was the best kind of person that ever was, Nathan."

"Then why did she get cancer and die?" Her lips tightened.

"Because she was human," she whispered. "There is no other reason." She ushered me out of my father's room. "Come on, go show me one of those cartwheel flip-flop things you do." She ran me outside and watched as I flipped from one side of the yard to the other, taking my mind off my mother's death for the moment.

Rachel picked up a letter and laughed, reading the letter written in crayon on a paper bag:

Dear Mommy
I don't like Nathan any mores so culd you send me anuther bruther from Heven? If you cant find one, a dog wuld be beter.

Love,
Rachel

I snatched the aged letter and looked at it.

"When did you write this?"

"Last year," she said, breaking into laughter.

Now that the holidays were in full swing, staff members took days off here or there, leaving the medical students to help out where necessary, seeing patients who weren't part of our normal rounds. Some of the medical students were even volunteered to help decorate certain floors of the hospital for Christmas. This was my assignment for the day, and I was grateful to get out of the emergency room for a while. Normally, Christmas would sneak up on me, leaving me in a lurch to find Christmas presents for everyone, but this year I couldn't wait. I hadn't been this excited about Christmas since before my mother died.

I filtered through the boxes of tinsel and bulbs and

helped Denise and Claudia spruce up the nurses' station on the pediatrics floor. I even hung tacky icicle lights from the ceiling so they'd dangle over the entire circumference of the desk.

"I'm going to leave those up till July," Denise said.

"So you're the neighbor in the apartment next to mine," I said, jumping off the ladder. I found a small tabletop tree in a box and pulled it onto the desk, straightening each limb. I was going to leave it at the nurses' station when a thought struck me. Digging through the boxes, I found a small string of lights and little bulbs that were perfect for the tree. I poked my head into Hope's room.

"Knock, knock." Hope looked up and motioned for me to come in. Her mother was sitting beside her on the bed. "Who'd like a little Christmas cheer in here?"

"Can I have that to myself?" she asked, looking at the small tree in my hands.

"You can have it, but you have to do the work." I put the tree on a cart and rolled it to Hope's bedside. Her mother helped her sit up and winked at me; Hope reached for the string of lights, sizing them up. I left to find a few other decorations.

"Playing favorites?" Denise asked. I stopped digging through a box by the nurses' station and looked up at her.

"Is this bad?" She pulled out a cheap, dancing Santa and handed it to me.

"If it is, I'm guilty, too. Take her whatever she'd like."

When I returned to Hope's room later in the day to check on her, I laughed out loud at the sight. There sat the tiny tree, drooping from the weight of ornaments; red ribbon hung from the lamps and tinsel surrounded the bed, window, door, and TV. A small wooden nativity sat on the bed stand next to Hope, and the Santa stood on the tabletop next to the tree, swinging his hips from side to side to "Rockin' Around the Christmas Tree."

"Denise kept coming back with things," her mother said.

"Couldn't she find any tacky plastic lawn ornaments?" I asked.

"She's still looking," Hope said, smiling.

The Sullivans dragged the large Douglas fir through the back door, and Jim grunted in satisfaction. "Now that's a man's tree. Isn't it, Luke?" Luke pulled off his coat and gloves and threw them on the floor.

"Yeahhh," Luke said, grunting like his father.

"Three whacks, and this baby was on the ground begging for mercy," Jim said, struggling to stand the tree up.

"Thirty whacks is more like it," Allison said. "The poor thing was saying, 'Please, just get it over with, already.' " Jim laughed although no one could see him through the tree's branches.

"When I stand it up, slip the tree stand under it." Meghan tried to help her father lift the tree, but she had

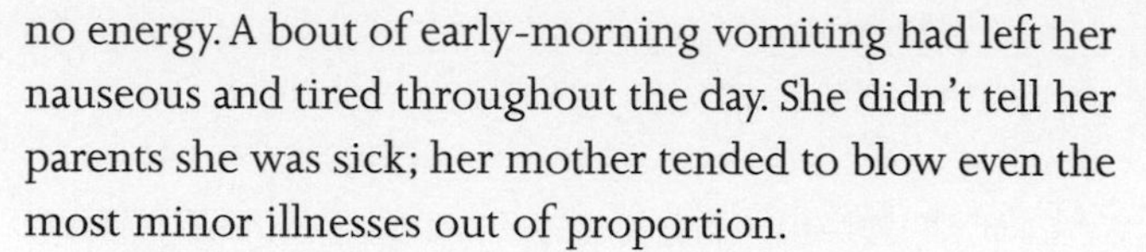

no energy. A bout of early-morning vomiting had left her nauseous and tired throughout the day. She didn't tell her parents she was sick; her mother tended to blow even the most minor illnesses out of proportion.

"We'll be finding pine needles in August," Allison said, bending over to put the stand in place.

"Before Christmas, Allison," Jim yelled through the mass of needles. "These things are killing me!"

Allison tightened the bolts on the stand, which started a verbal volley of *lean it to the left, more to the right, it's leaning backward now, turn it toward the window, turn it away from the window, back it up, pull it forward, more, more, more, no, move it back again.*

When the tree was all but decorated, Jim hoisted Olivia into the air to place the angel on the top branch, which just missed the ceiling. Olivia stretched her small arms to the upper reaches of the tree. "She's beautiful," Olivia said, pulling her shirt back down to cover her belly. Jim turned off all the lights, and the family sat together on the sofa, admiring their work.

"We should sell tickets for people to come see it," Meghan said, exhausted from the effort.

Allison raised her cup of cider. "Here's to the official beginning of another Sullivan family Christmas. May it be the most beautiful one ever!"

• • •

At one in the morning, Meghan woke her mother and father. When Jim turned on the light and saw her face, he swept her up in his arms and ran to the car.

The ER was quiet. Rory was on duty. He paused when he looked at Meghan; her skin and eyes were yellow in color. "I think I have food poisoning," Meghan said. "It's either that or the worst flu I've ever had." Rory took her temperature, and she was running a high fever. His physical exam revealed that her liver was enlarged and felt firm to the touch.

"We need to do some blood work," Rory said. Meghan groaned.

"Dr. Goetz just drew blood a few days ago. Can't you just read those results?" Rory shook his head.

"You probably weren't jaundiced a few days ago."

"I'm sorry you had to wait so long," Rory said, pulling open the curtain. Another doctor was with him. "But I wanted Dr. Lucas, one of our gastroenterologists, to read these results, as well as one of our infectious disease specialists."

Allison and Jim were quiet, staring at Rory and Dr. Lucas.

"I'm Dr. Lucas." Meghan shook the doctor's hand. "Your blood tests revealed that your hepatic enzymes are elevated." Meghan sat still, looking at her. "We'd like to do a needle biopsy of your liver to rule out hepatitis."

"When?" Meghan asked.

"Right away."

Dr. Lucas clutched Meghan's file to her chest and walked into the room where Jim, Allison, and Meghan had been waiting for the last few hours for the biopsy reports from pathology. "The biopsy is showing an undifferentiated hepatitis."

"What is that?" Meghan asked. Dr. Lucas paused and took a breath.

"You have something that is causing your liver to be inflamed. Normally we can identify that as hepatitis A, B, or C; but in your case we can't identify the cause." Meghan and her parents sat in silence, trying to grasp what Dr. Lucas was saying.

"She hasn't done anything to get hepatitis," Jim said. Her illness just didn't make sense.

"This is a viral hepatitis," Dr. Lucas said. "Meghan saw Dr. Goetz six months ago for her annual exam and told him she'd been feeling nauseous previous to that but that it eventually went away." Meghan nodded. "I would speculate that that is when the hepatitis was affecting your liver."

"But where did it come from?" Allison asked.

"We can't determine what the infectious agent was. It

could be a million things. It could have been anything airborne."

"What will you do?" Jim asked. Dr. Lucas hated this part of her job. She held tighter to the file and looked at Meghan.

"Judging by your biopsy, this is progressing at a rapid pace, and we need to get a transplant surgeon involved with your care immediately." Meghan felt her heart drop but never took her eyes off Dr. Lucas. "I've contacted a transplant surgeon to speak with you as soon as possible." Allison jumped to her feet.

"Oh God, no," she wailed. "There must be something else you can do."

"This is the only thing we can do," Dr. Lucas said.

My rotation started at six; I figured I'd call Meghan later in the morning, once I knew she was up. At ten, I reached for the phone on the nurses' station in the ER but stopped dialing when a folder in a stack of files caught my eye. Meghan's name was on it. I scanned it and snapped my head up, looking for Rory. He was in the lounge, getting his things together to go home. He was still answering my questions as I bounded up the stairs.

. . .

"Here I am," Meghan said. "Back at my favorite vacation destination." I glanced at Jim and Allison, who looked like they'd logged ten years in the last nine hours.

I snatched her chart at the end of her bed and glanced over it, feeling my heart beat faster as I read the notes Dr. Lucas had written: *vital signs stable, patient condition jaundiced and deteriorating. Biopsy report shows fulminant hepatitis.* I could hear myself breathing—full-blown hepatitis. Then I read, *Consult transplant team.* Meghan watched me read through the notes. "It's not as bad as they say," she said, trying to smile. It felt as if the wind had been knocked out of me and I couldn't speak. I kept staring at the chart—*fulminant hepatitis.* Meghan motioned for me to sit on the side of her bed.

"Dr. Lucas said there's the possibility of finding a living donor." I nodded. Since the liver regenerates itself, a portion is all that is necessary for a successful transplant. Jim and Allison's hopes would soon be dashed when they learned that neither of them, nor extended family members, were a close enough match. I immediately went through the tests and would learn later that even Dr. Goetz was tested. None of us came close enough to matching.

"You doctors are always so serious," Meghan said, comforting *me.* She grabbed my hand and held it tight. "You always forget that Christmas is full of miracles." I looked up at her. "There's always a miracle at Christmas," she said.

A thick, dry knot formed in my throat. I knew otherwise. How many times did I pray for a miracle? How many times did I beg God to heal my mother and make her well? I knew that miracles still happened, but I also knew that sometimes it was as if the heavens were silent.

EIGHT

Hope, like faith, is nothing if it is not courageous;
it is nothing if it is not ridiculous.
—Thornton Wilder

Dr. Goetz pushed a wheelchair to Meghan's room.

"For m'lady," he said.

"I can walk, Dr. Goetz," she said. He pointed to the chair.

"Hospital policy. Sit."

"Don't you have orderlies who do this?" she asked.

"You want an orderly to take out my best girl," Dr. Goetz said, teasing her. "I don't think so!" He pushed her through the halls and into the elevator. Jim pulled the car around, and Dr. Goetz pushed Meghan to the curb, opening the car door for her. He helped her out of the chair and held on to her, afraid she might fall on the melted snow on the pavement.

"I can walk on my own, Dr. Goetz," she said.

"I know you can," he said. "But I might fall."

He smiled and helped her into the car. Then he did something he'd never done with any of his patients: he

kissed her forehead. He closed the door, and Meghan waved at him through the window. He felt a catch in his throat and put his head down to avoid eye contact with anyone who might stop him to talk; then he pushed the chair back into the hospital.

I made it through my rounds but it felt as if I were walking through a long tunnel of a dream that wouldn't end, but I was confident that I'd awaken and learn that the doctors had made a mistake: Meghan wasn't sick after all. I can't remember how many times I told myself that when my mother was ill, but it should have been enough to learn by now that Meghan was sick. In a little while, if she didn't get a transplant, she would get very sick. After my rounds, I made my way to the lounge and tried to open my locker. It was jammed. I jiggled the handle and pulled it toward me, but the locker wouldn't budge. In frustration I tried several times. I leaned my head on the locker. *This isn't happening again*. I lifted the handle. Nothing. In anger I beat my fists into the locker and pounded it over and over and over. *Why did I meet her?* I couldn't go through it again. I couldn't watch someone I love get weaker every day until death finally snatched her away.

In one of her letters my mother wrote,

Life never has and never will be fair, Nathan. I won't be the first person you lose; there will be others. You'll stand by their

side as they lie dying or beside their grave in a cemetery and it's there that you'll have to make a decision. You can either lean into God or turn away. It will always be your choice, Nathan, not His.

I closed my eyes. She never turned away. Even in death, my mother chose to go through the pain with God rather than without Him. I didn't know if I could make that same decision.

There are days when I can remember everything Meghan and I did together over the next three weeks, then there are days when I can't remember anything at all. She would turn off all the lights in her family's living room, leaving only the lights on the tree to light up the room, and we'd sit there for hours and talk about everything or we'd watch the lights on the tree and say nothing at all. Sometimes, we'd drive to the park and walk around the lake. Each time we were there Meghan would look for the runner she used to pace herself against, but we never saw her. "It's the wrong time of day," she would say, disappointed. "I hope I get to see her again." Neither of us knew if she would—her body was reminding us every day that time was short.

One day our walk around the lake was slower than usual. I held firm to Meghan's hand, afraid she would slip on the patches of ice on the path. She stopped

beneath the giant oak tree and looked out over the frozen water. She loved it there. She looked from side to side, taking it all in as if it were the first time she'd seen it. We stood in silence as she watched the runners making their way around the perimeter of the lake, and I knew she'd give anything to be running with them.

My mother wrote in her last letter to me:

Dear Nathan,
You have grown so fast. It was only yesterday your father and I brought you home from the hospital. As I watched you grow into the fine little man you are, I was reminded time and again that life is a mist. We're here for a while and then we just fade away, leaving little bits of ourselves behind for the people we love. You'll be a man like your daddy before you know it and I hope that when you're grown that you won't let life slip by. I hope that for every loop and drop this roller coaster takes you on, that you'll keep hanging on for the rest of the ride. Just know that the ride is over before you know it and if you close your eyes, you'll miss it.

I didn't want to miss a second of the ride with Meghan.

Meghan woke to sounds of her mother in the kitchen. She tiptoed through the living room and stuck her head around the corner: Allison was making every effort to be quiet, closing cabinets and removing bowls and pans with care. "What are you doing, Mom?" Meghan asked. Allison jumped at her voice.

"Don't scare me, Meghan; I'm getting too old. Did I wake you?"

"No. What are you making?"

"Peanut butter fudge." It was Luke's favorite. Her mother made it every year for Christmas, along with date balls for Jim, cookies by the dozen for Olivia and her class, and homemade candy that took an hour to beat to perfection for Meghan. Meghan ran back toward her room.

"I'm going to change and come help you." Allison stopped her.

"I can do it, Meg. Just lie on the couch and rest." Meghan stopped in the hallway and turned back to her mother. For days her mom and dad had walked on eggshells around her. Meghan was tired of it.

"Would you stop treating me like a baby, Mom?"

"I wasn't. I was trying to treat you like normal." Allison wanted to treat her as she always did, but things were different now and she no longer knew how to act or what to do.

"Well, you're not, Mom. If you were, you'd talk about what's happening." Allison stuck her head in the refrigerator. "See, you're avoiding it right now!" Allison pulled out a pound of butter and set it on the counter. "Mom, look at me." Allison clutched the recipe box and looked at Meghan. "A transplant might never become available."

Tears pooled in Allison's eyes. "Don't say that, Meghan."

"Mom, you heard the doctors. I either get a transplant or . . ." Tears fell down Allison's face as she cut Meghan off.

"Please don't say that, Meghan," she whispered. "I can't think about . . ." She couldn't finish. She picked up a dishcloth and buried her face in it.

"Mom, if I die, you can't be sad forever." Allison didn't respond. "You're going to look out the window and life will still go on. That's just how it is." Allison wanted to say it was a whole lot more than that for the people who were left behind, but she remained quiet. "Do you know what I want more than anything, Mom?" Allison looked up.

"What?"

"I want to help you make peanut butter fudge." Allison tried to laugh and handed Meghan a bowl.

They spent the morning talking and laughing as one Christmas treat after another was prepared. When Meghan lay down to rest after lunch, Allison cleaned up the mess in the kitchen, turning the TV news up to drown out the sound of her crying.

Meghan pulled a folder containing information about the scholarship run out of her desk in the bedroom. She sat Jim and Allison down, going over every last detail

from how she wanted the sponsorships organized to the day of the run itself. "We're doing this awfully early, aren't we," Jim said. "Isn't the race in June?"

"Dad, it has to be organized so we'll know what else needs to be done."

"Besides my bank account, where else is all the money going once you collect it?" Jim asked, hoping to make Meghan laugh. She was all business.

"That's where I need help. Once the money goes into a trust we're going to need a lawyer or somebody to help us make all this legal." Meghan wrote the word "lawyer" on her legal pad and circled it. She'd have to find a lawyer she could trust.

They finished the work an hour later, and Meghan put everything back into her folder. "I want Charlie to be the first recipient," she said. She looked at her mom and dad. "It's important to me that somebody know that."

I pulled into Meghan's drive after my rounds one day and saw Charlie sitting on the swing set in the backyard. It was so cold, the snow crunched beneath me as I walked toward him. I zipped my jacket and sat on the swing next to him.

"It's awfully cold out here," I said.

"I don't mind it," he said, watching his feet dig into the snow as he twisted the swing from side to side. I stuck my hands in my pockets.

“Did you visit with Meghan?” He nodded. “How was it?” He shrugged his shoulders.

“Will they find a transplant?” His voice was soft. I barely heard the question.

“As soon as a match is available, they’ll get her to the hospital.”

“But will they find one?” I paused, looking out over the white yard.

“I don’t know.” He nodded and leaned farther over the swing, staring at his feet.

“Why aren’t more people organ donors?”

“I don’t know. Afraid that if they actually say they are that something will happen to them; as if they’re inviting death into their home.”

“That’s stupid,” he said. “People are dying every day because they need a kidney or liver or a new heart.” He stopped swaying back and forth and looked at me. “She says there are always miracles at Christmas. Do you believe that?” My heart sank. I didn’t want to answer him, but I knew there was no way around it. Charlie was too smart for double-talk.

“If we can’t believe that miracles happen, then we may as well stop believing anything at all.” He looked down at the ground again.

“Do you love her?” he asked. He waited for me to answer.

“Man to man?” I asked.

“Man to man.”

“Yes.”

“Then you better tell her soon because I love her, too, and if you don’t tell her, I will.”

I smiled. Charlie was a rare gem. I reached over and squeezed the back of his neck, praying that the miracle Meghan believed in would happen soon.

NINE

A miracle, my friend, is an event which creates faith.

—George Bernard Shaw

Meghan was lying on the sofa; nausea had hit her hard that morning, and she had vomited right before everyone came to visit. Charlie sat on a chair with two of Meghan's teammates, who were perched on each arm of the chair. Leslie grinned as he turned three shades of red when one of the girls would flirt with him, teasing him about being Meghan's secret coach.

"Does she rub your head before she runs?" one of them asked, rubbing Charlie's head and messing up his hair.

"Or does she kiss you?" another asked, turning and kissing Charlie on the cheek. His eyes widened, and Leslie stepped into the kitchen before he saw her laughing.

Before Meghan let the girls leave she grilled them about how much money they were raising for the race. "Trust me," Michele said. "They're all working hard.

You're going to raise more money for this run than you ever imagined."

Meghan's teammates filed out the door, rubbing Charlie's head for good luck. As soon as the winter break was over they'd all be at practice again and told Meghan they expected her there.

Meghan was quiet. Everyone was always so cheerful, taking great strides to step around any questions about her illness. With the exception of the first, *How do you feel?* nobody asked anything else. Nobody, that is, except Charlie. He walked to the sofa and sat down beside Meghan.

"Are you getting sicker every day?"

Meghan knew she'd have to tell him the truth. "Yes."

He was quiet. "When will you have to go back to the hospital?"

"I don't know," she said, but she knew it would be soon.

Allison and Leslie sat in the family room listening as Meghan laughed and visited with Charlie and her friends. "All these years I've been so worried about her heart," Allison said. "I never dreamed anything like this would happen." Tears fell down her face, and Leslie squeezed her hand. "I should have known her heart wouldn't give out. She's always had more heart than any of us." Leslie stayed quiet and listened; she knew there

was nothing she could say. She could try saying something like, *A liver will be available soon*, but she didn't know that. "Sometimes I try to prepare myself," Allison whispered. She stopped. "I try to prepare for the day when . . ."

"There's nothing to prepare for, Allison. She's still here." A tear fell down Allison's cheek, and she brushed it away.

"Every day I look at her and say, 'Oh God, please! Please save my little girl's life.' " She covered her face and wept, letting her tears fall in her hands. Leslie touched her arm.

"She's still here, Allison. She's looking at you and Jim and loving you every day, and while she's doing that there's still hope. She's still here," Leslie said. Allison nodded and tears fell from her chin.

"But for how long," Allison whispered.

Leslie and Charlie pulled on their coats to leave. "You need to keep your eyes on the finish line," Charlie said, cracking his knuckles. "Don't ever take your eyes off the goal because your miracle's coming. I just know it." Meghan grabbed his hands.

"Stop doing that," she said. "Your fingers are going to look like breadsticks." Allison and Leslie watched at the door, smiling. Given their ages, Charlie and Meghan were the most unlikely of friends, but both women knew there

was a deep bond between them. Meghan hugged Charlie. “Thanks for coming over today,” she said in his ear.

“I’ll come by every day,” he said. He put his head down and wouldn’t look at her. “You’re my best friend, Meghan.” He darted for the door before she could respond.

“I want to get tested to see if I can be a donor for Meghan,” Charlie said, on the drive home. Leslie looked at him; she knew he was serious.

“I know you love Meghan, but you just can’t do that, Charlie. Your heart would never make it through the surgery.”

“I knew you’d say that,” he said, snapping his head to stare out the passenger window.

“Dr. Goetz would never let you,” Leslie said. “You know that.” Charlie wasn’t listening. “Meghan wouldn’t let you, either.” He turned to look at his mother. “You know that, too.” Charlie remained quiet.

“Mom?” Leslie looked at him. “For weeks I haven’t been able to pray for Meghan’s miracle because I knew that somebody would have to die. I mean, if a living donor wasn’t found.” He looked at his mother. “But we have to pray for that now. Somebody has to die, or Meghan will.”

. . .

I got to Meghan's late one day. I was doing the workup of a patient that took longer than expected, and I could hear time tick away in my ears as one thing after another kept me at the hospital for another hour. I walked into her house and found her on the sofa.

"Would you take me to the park?" she asked. I drove to the park and opened my door, but she stopped me. "I just want to look at it," she said, watching ice-skaters on the lake. She looked at the small gazebo on the other side of the lake. Someone had decorated it for Christmas with huge red bows, swags of spruce, and bright colored lights. Snow clung to colored bulbs that covered a huge evergreen in the middle of the park. "I can't believe it's almost Christmas," she said. She was quiet as she watched two runners make their way past my truck and around the lake. "Was your mother afraid when she died?"

The question took me off guard. "No."

She kept watching the runners.

"When you think about her now, do you remember the way she died or how she lived?"

"How she lived."

She nodded. She watched as runners made one loop after another around the lake. Tears filled her eyes and made their way down her face and over her chin, spilling onto her hands. "I'm never going to run again," she said, wiping her face. "It's funny how you draw up a plan for your life." Her voice was stronger now. "Then something happens that proves you wrong." She was crying harder,

and I pulled her to me, wrapping my arms around her. "You're reminded that you only have a few years: eighty, maybe sixty-five . . . or nineteen." Her shoulders were shaking. "I don't want to leave my family," she said, sobbing. "I don't want to leave you, Nathan." She was grabbing my face, searching my eyes.

"We have to hold on for your miracle, Meg," I said, holding on to her. I opened my door and slid her off the seat, into my arms. I walked down the slope leading to the path around the lake and started to carry her around it.

"What are you doing?" she asked. I pulled her closer and picked up my pace, running. A few runners ran off to the side, staring as I ran with Meghan in my arms. She lifted an arm up toward the sky and squinted into the sun, feeling the wind on her face. She smiled; she was running around the lake she loved.

TEN

Only a life lived for others is the life worthwhile.

—Albert Einstein

Meghan was admitted to the hospital on a Thursday. Her condition was declining, so physicians would no longer permit her to stay home. Doctors would keep her as comfortable as possible and do everything they could to keep her from catching even a common cold. They had to keep her as healthy as possible. Allison held on to Olivia's hand and walked with her and Luke down the hall, toward Meghan's room.

"Is Dr. Goetz keeping you here again?" Olivia asked, jumping onto Meghan's bed. Meghan shook her head and motioned for Luke to come closer, then, making things as clear as possible, she told them everything.

I had planned to stay at my dad's for Christmas break, but when Meghan got sick I decided to stay in my apartment, closer to the hospital. I finished up my rounds on

the twenty-third and gathered my things to leave. Peter Vashti saw me in the cafeteria. I hadn't seen him since he helped get me out of the rotation with Dr. Goetz. We talked about Meghan, and I shared with him my decision to leave medical school. He had seen several of his own classmates drop out during their third year, so what I said didn't take him by surprise.

"I think it's going to be hard for you to walk away," Peter said. He leaned forward in his seat and looked me in the eye. "Don't make this decision because things got tough for a while. You'll go through rough times again. There were doctors that I hated during my third year."

I smiled at Peter. I knew what he was thinking. "I haven't made my decision because of Dr. Goetz or any other doctor. I just know that some of you are meant to be doctors, and some of us aren't."

"Or maybe some kept working through the tough times while some bowed out. I know that some of my classmates regret the decision they made. I just hope you won't."

I didn't have time to dwell on what Peter said. I pulled my things together, said good-bye to everyone, and walked out the doors leading to the parking lot. They closed behind me and I stopped. It felt so final, as if they were closing forever, but I couldn't take the time to think about that. Not now anyway.

. . .

I visited Meghan when Allison took Luke and Olivia home. I sat down on the side of her bed and could feel that something was wrong. She wasn't looking at me. I reached for her hand, but she moved it onto her chest. For the last two days it felt as if she was distancing herself from me. I started to speak. "Are you . . ." She turned toward me; tears were on her face.

"I can't do this to you," she said.

"Do what?" I asked, confused.

"I can't put you through this again." Tears streamed down her face now.

"Meghan . . ."

"You're not going to sit around and wait for me to die like you did your mother. Nobody deserves to go through that again." She turned her face away and I tried to turn it toward me but she resisted. "Please go, Nathan." I turned her face with my hands and looked at her.

"What are you talking about? Let me decide what I should or shouldn't do."

"I don't want you to come see me here. It's too hard!" She was sobbing. Jim ran into the room and looked at us. "Daddy, please make Nathan leave." Jim squeezed my shoulder as I walked out the door.

I drove the hour to my dad's. He and Gramma weren't expecting me. Gramma was already in bed for the night. Dad made a pot of coffee and sat across the table from me. I was so tired I could have put my head on the table and slept there for the night.

I avoided eye contact. I knew if I looked at my dad that my emotions would unravel, and I didn't want that to happen. I held the cup between my hands and swirled the black liquid up one side and down the other.

"How's Meghan?" Dad asked.

"Not good. She's getting weaker." I paused. Dad didn't ask a lot of questions or offer up what my grandmother called "bubbles of hope," a statement that is as solid as a bubble. We heard lots of them when my mother was sick: *Maggie's going to lick this*, someone would say to my father, or *Everything's going to be all right, Nathan*. Dad had lived long enough to know that Meghan might not be all right.

"How are you?" he asked.

I bit the inside of my mouth and nodded. I tried to hold back the tears. I tried to suck it up and hold it together. "She said she doesn't want to see me again." My voice was so small. "She said she can't put me through it again."

"Can you go through it again?" Dad asked. I didn't look up at him.

"Yes," I whispered.

"Then that's where you need to be." I kept my eyes on the table.

"Dad," I said, "do you think it's possible to fall in love after knowing someone for only a couple of months?"

"I fell in love with your mother the first day I met her," he said. "So a couple of months seems long to me."

"I just keep wondering why I met her," I said, squeezing the cup between my hands. "Why did I have to meet her?"

"Because you were supposed to love her," Dad said. His words struck me hard. Was I supposed to meet Meghan for no other reason than to love her as she died? I felt my shoulders shaking. Tears were on my face, but I was silent. Dad pulled my head into his chest and I grabbed on to him, sobbing.

"Love her while you can," he said, bending low to my ear. "Love her as long as you can."

I drove to my apartment and pulled out the letters from my mother. I glanced through them and found the one I was looking for.

Dear Nathan,

One day, maybe in a few months, or a few years, you'll start to look at women (maybe a friend's mother or someone you work with) and wonder why I couldn't have lived to be as old as she is. You'll wish that I could be there with you to meet a girlfriend or fix your tie on your wedding day or hold your children, but don't dwell on the pain. Focus on the happiness that you feel on those days and the happiness that I had as your mother. If I was given another five, ten, or forty years, I don't think I could be happier than I was during these 34 years because it's not about how long you live but how you live and who you love and I loved you. More than you'll ever know.

I felt tears run down my nose and across my cheeks. I had long since resigned myself to the fact that my mother's words would bring tears to my eyes for the rest of my life. She went on:

The pain you feel now will help you care for others, Nathan. It will help you love them through the hardest times. Always remember that Love wins. Remember when we looked at the valley together on top of the ridge last year? Regardless of the pain or sorrow you go through in the valley, there will always be love at the end. It may be hard to walk through, but God will use your time there for good. I know He will.

I folded the letter, slipping it back inside the envelope, and grabbed my keys.

The ICU was quiet. Meghan had been asleep for hours. I saw Jim sitting in a chair in the waiting room; he was half-asleep. I walked toward him, and he opened his eyes when he heard my footsteps. I sat down beside him. "She can say whatever she wants, but I'm not going anywhere," I said. Jim clapped my shoulder and rested his hand there. Sometime in the early-morning hours, we both drifted to sleep.

I stirred when I heard a nurse on the phone giving her husband a detailed list of what to buy at the grocery store. Jim was still asleep; his neck bent back in a tortuous position. I walked to Meghan's room and looked inside. Allison was asleep on a bed shoved against the wall. I crept inside and stood next to Meghan. She turned toward me and opened her eyes.

"Just so you know," I said, whispering. "I'm just as stubborn as you are, and I'm not going anywhere." She was too tired to argue. She smiled and fell back to sleep.

Someone was always with Meghan; sometimes two or three of us were in the room at the same time, the nurses disregarding hospital policy regarding the number of ICU visitors. "Are we driving you crazy," Allison asked, brushing Meghan's hair off her face. Megan smiled; she was getting too tired to sit up, let alone speak. She fell asleep and Allison and Jim slipped out of the room. They were never gone long. They would take just enough time to cry alone in the bathroom or wander the halls, hoping to find a miracle hidden in the cracks of the floor or behind a door.

I sat beside Meghan and held her hand. *Is this what it was like for my dad? Did he watch my mother sleep for hours during the last days of her life?* Meghan opened her eyes and smiled. "I dreamed we were dancing again," she said. "We were in the waiting room and it was decorated for Christmas and

I was wearing a gold, silk dress this time, not some cheap doctor's jacket." I laughed.

"Hey, it was all I could afford at the time." She smiled and closed her eyes; she was dreaming again.

Jim pulled the small, fake tree through the door and set it on a rolling cart in Meghan's room. Olivia followed, carrying two big bags that were bigger than her, and Luke had strings of lights hanging around his neck. Jim put up his hands when he saw the look on Allison's face.

"No pine needles with this one," he said. They decorated the tree while Meghan watched, and Jim hauled in a huge plastic bag filled with presents. Christmas was two days away.

Charlie and Leslie dropped by later in the morning. Meghan pointed out a gift under the tree, and Charlie picked it up. "Open it," she said. "It's for you."

"But I don't have anything for you," he said. "That's not fair."

"Don't argue on Christmas Eve. Just open it." Charlie tore the paper and pulled out several ribbons and trophies. "For my coach," she said, watching Charlie's eyes.

"Why are you giving me all your trophies and ribbons?"

"You were the one who annoyed me so much and

made all those impossible demands like 'take two more seconds off. No, I changed my mind, take ten.' " Charlie raised his eyebrows and smiled.

"I just try to do my job." He sat on the edge of her bed and grew quiet. "It's coming, isn't it?"

"What?" Meghan asked.

"Your Christmas miracle."

"I hope so," she said.

"I know so," Charlie said. Meghan smiled. Charlie so wanted to believe in miracles, wanted to be a part of one. She looked at Leslie and hoped she and Rich would one day be able to explain things to him. She pulled Charlie's face toward hers and gave him a kiss. He wiped it off.

"Why do you girls keep kissing me?" he said, rubbing his face.

I didn't know if we'd get any time alone on Christmas Day, so when Jim took Luke and Olivia home for the day and Allison slipped away to the cafeteria, I handed Meghan her gift.

"Yours is under the tree," she said. I found it: a small box covered with red paper.

"Open yours first," I said. She ran her finger under the tape and pulled at the wrapping. Her mouth opened when she saw it. "I saw it hanging in a store window."

I was walking toward Gunther's Sports in my hometown to pick up some new fishing equipment for Dad's Christmas present. It had just started to snow, and the wind had picked up, so I put my head down. I glanced

up only a moment to say hello to someone in front of Wilson's Department Store when something caught my eye in the window. I walked closer and stared. *How did it get here of all places?*

I ran inside and a clerk lifted it out of the window and handed it to me. I tried to make out the name in the corner but couldn't. I flipped it over, hoping to find the information there.

"Who painted this?" I asked the clerk. She shrugged her shoulders. I kept staring at it. It was beautiful, painted to perfection down to the last detail: the giant oak, with snow clinging to every limb, the lake was frozen over, you could just make out footprints on the path surrounding it, and even the gazebo was there, decorated for Christmas.

"This park is an hour away," I said to the clerk. "Who brought this here to sell?" She shrugged again, mumbling something about how Wilson's didn't even sell paintings, let alone one by some unknown artist.

"It's so beautiful," Meghan said, holding the painting in her hands. She arched her brows and looked at the gift in my hand. I tore into the paper and opened the small box. There was a runner's wrist stopwatch inside. I read the card she had tucked under the bow.

In case you can't find someone to pace yourself with. I smiled and pulled out the watch, holding it in my hand. I leaned down and kissed her. "I found someone to pace myself with," I said.

It was there, in the quiet of her hospital room as she

held on to a painting of the park she adored, that I told Meghan I loved her.

On Christmas morning I watched as the Sullivans unwrapped one gift after another, and it seemed everyone, including Meghan, forgot she was ill. Jim waded through the sea of wrapping paper and pulled out the last of the gifts: coloring books that Santa left for Olivia, a remote-controlled car for Luke, and a lone gift sitting at the back of the tree with Meghan's name on it. "One more gift," he said, handing it to her.

"No name on it. This one must be from Santa," Meghan said, taking the gift from her father. She unwrapped the green foil, pulled back the tissue paper, and saw a beautiful silver frame with a stained-glass star on each side. She stared at the picture inside, one of the night sky twinkling with thousands of stars.

"Just in case you get too busy at Stanford or Georgetown to go out and look at them," Jim said, "you can hold this up and we'll still be looking at them together." Meghan smiled, holding the picture. "You're still my star," Jim whispered, kissing her. "You'll always be my star."

Leslie Bennett drove ten-year-old Matthew to her mother and father's house. They were supposed to spend the morning with her parents after opening gifts at their

own house, but Charlie still wasn't awake at seven and Matthew could barely contain himself; he just had to get at those presents. At seven-thirty, Leslie checked on Charlie, and he was still sound asleep. Since they could no longer take Matthew's pleading, Leslie pulled on her coat and decided to drive Matthew to her parents' house; at least he could open a couple of gifts there. Maybe that would appease him until Charlie woke up. Matt was already beside himself over a gift Charlie had received yesterday at the hospital.

While Charlie was visiting Meghan, Denise had come down from pediatrics with a gift for him. His eyes lit up when he opened up an envelope with a certificate inside.

"Good for four tickets to the WWF in August," Charlie read, excited. "Is this real?"

"It's real." Denise squeezed his arm and turned to go.

"You didn't have to get him anything," Leslie said, moved by Denise's kindness. So many of the hospital staff knew that Charlie's medical bills had been a strain on the Bennetts and had been so kind over the years, giving him gifts on his birthday and Christmas.

"I know he loves it. I heard it was coming, so I just had to get them." Leslie felt a catch in her throat, but she managed to hug Denise and wish her a merry Christmas. Matthew was as excited about the gift as Charlie.

Rich rinsed out the dishes from breakfast and started to unload the dishwasher when he heard a knock at the

door. Before he could dry his hands and get to the living room, whoever had knocked was already gone. He opened the door and saw a plain white envelope sticking to the door with a large red bow attached to it. He ripped it open and pulled out one thousand dollars in cash. Rich ran into the yard and spun around in all directions, looking for a car or anyone in the street. He bolted into the house to call Leslie, and as he was telling her what happened he heard another knock at the door. He threw the phone down on the counter and ran to the door. Again, no one was there but another envelope with a bow swayed in the cold air. Rich snatched it off and ran into the yard again, spinning on his heels. He opened it and breathlessly counted another wad of money as Leslie listened. "One thousand dollars," he shouted into the phone. Tears filled Leslie's eyes.

"What's going on?" she whispered.

"I don't know," Rich shouted. "I don't know!" Then there was another rap at the door. "There's another knock!" He threw the phone down and raced to the door, throwing it open and running to the yard before anyone could get away but again, there was no one there. He snatched the envelope from the door. His heart pounded as he picked up the phone. "It's another envelope, Les." His hands shook as he opened it and the money fell to the counter. "It's more money," he said, choking on the words. "It's *two* thousand dollars." Leslie

cried on the other end. Meghan was right; Christmas was the season for miracles. There was just enough money to help them pay off bills that had accumulated over the past two months. Leslie sat down and held the phone to her ear, crying. They racked their brains trying to imagine who might have done such a thing. Everyone—people from the hospital to Charlie's school and their neighbors—had already been so good to them. They would never know who left the money so they could thank them, but sometimes giving is all the thanks that some people ever need.

Charlie visited Meghan in the afternoon, bringing a framed picture of the two of them together, taken after one of her cross-country meets. "I should have known the best gift would be from you," she said, making him smile. As they talked, Meghan drifted off to sleep; Charlie looked up at me, frightened. I led him down the hall, into the waiting room.

"It's the medications, Charlie," I said, trying to ease his mind. He was quiet for the longest time.

"Do you think she'd run through the gates of Heaven? Or would that be the wrong thing to do?"

"I think you can probably go through the gates any way you like." He thought for a moment.

"Then I'd definitely run through them." He smiled, looking at me. "It'd be the only time I ever ran without having to sit down and rest." I put my hand around his shoulder. We sat quietly, and I could hear the clock ticking on the wall in front of me. It's strange how deafening time can be when you want it to slow down.

Charlie waited for Meghan to wake up, then Leslie took another picture of Charlie sitting on Meghan's bed, Meghan's arm slung over his shoulder.

"Are you going to hover around my bed all day?" Meghan asked late in the afternoon. I threw my hands in the air.

"Are you trying to get rid of me again?" She reached for my hand.

"Please go be with your family for a while." I sat down next to her.

"They know I'm here."

"But it's Christmas! Please go wish your grandmother a merry Christmas in person. It's only an hour away . . . thirty minutes the way you drive. Please go see them. There's nothing for you to do here, anyway."

"She's stubborn like her mother," Jim said. "There's no reasoning with either one of them." He put his hand on my back. "Why don't you take a break and go be with your family?" Everything in me said I shouldn't go, that I should just stay put; but Meghan was adamant.

"You can go eat dinner with your family and be back here by ten."

"I'll be back by eight."

“You can’t drive there, eat, open presents, and be back here by eight. Ten o’clock.”

“Nine.” I leaned down and I kissed her. “I love you,” I said. She held my face and looked me in the eyes.

“I love you, too. Now leave.”

When someone you love dies on a holiday, that day’s never the same again. My father and grandmother did everything they could to make Christmas special for me and Rachel, and my memories of each Christmas are filled with lots of food and family filling the next several days with nothing but laughter and boisterous conversation. But in the middle of it all, I would catch my father holding his coffee mug and staring out the window. Even as a child I knew he was thinking of my mother. Or I could hear Gramma humming or talking to herself, but then the kitchen would grow quiet and I’d catch a glimpse of her staring at a bowl or the recipe box and I knew she was remembering working with Mom to prepare the Christmas meal. The kitchen would be silent for several minutes; then I’d hear her blowing her nose before the humming started again.

As we grew older, Christmas became a quiet celebration. Gramma would travel to visit her two remaining children, my aunt Kathy and uncle Brian, while Dad, Rachel, and I celebrated together. Because of medical problems, Gramma hadn’t traveled the last couple of

Christmases. I had hoped Meghan would be part of our celebration this year. I shook my head. I couldn't believe I let her talk me into leaving the hospital. On the way to my father's house, I took a turn leading to the cemetery.

Our family visited my mother's grave every Christmas, but for whatever reason I decided to swing by there first before going home. I pulled onto the grounds and realized there was no way my little pickup was going to make it up the icy road that wound through the property. I parked and grabbed the sack off the front seat.

I hoofed my way up the road to my mother's tombstone and found it covered with ice. All the stones were sparkling from the most recent ice storm. I put the sack down and started clearing the leaves and debris from the stone. I caught movement in my eye and looked up to see a man carrying a wreath and poinsettias. We said hello to each other, and I think I wished him a merry Christmas, I don't know, I can't recall. He went about his business, carrying on with his work as I finished mine.

"I brought the shoes, Mom," I said, opening the sack and placing the glittery, beaded pair on her tombstone. "I know you don't need them anymore. Makes me feel better, though." The wind picked up, and I pulled my coat up around my neck and pushed the university hat I was wearing farther down on my head. "I've met a girl, Mom. And she's one of those girls you told me about; one I can't live without." My throat tightened, and I ran my fingers over the letters on the stone. "I can't imagine my life without her in it now."

The wind shrieked and drowned out my voice. I remembered my grandmother said she'd have dinner ready at 6:00. I looked down at my watch: 4:35. "I think I'm supposed to be eating Christmas dinner right now, but I'm not sure because the watch you bought for me doesn't work." I tapped the face of it and the second hand started to move. "But I can't get rid of it." I positioned the shoes so the light caught them, reflecting off the sequins just so. "I wish you were here with us, Mom. I'll wish that for the rest of my life."

Gramma pulled me inside the door, taking my coat from me. She held on to my face and studied my eyes before she gave me a kiss. "You didn't have to come," she said.

"Meg made me come." Her eyes filled with tears, and she kissed me again. After my mother died, words never had to be spoken to bring tears to Gramma's eyes.

I tried to eat my plateful of turkey and stuffing and mashed potatoes and peas, but I couldn't help but think I'd done something terrible in leaving the hospital. In my heart, I knew I should have stayed. We set the dishes aside and unwrapped our gifts by the tree. Rachel and I got Gramma a red silk wrap similar to the one she gave Mom on her last Christmas. Gramma had worn it when she was married and from the time she was a little girl, Mom

had wanted it. Gramma pulled the wrap from the box and ran it through her fingers.

"What in the world will I do with something this beautiful? It looks like something the queen of England would wear."

"Then wear it while you and the queen are having lunch," Dad said.

"I wouldn't know what to feed the queen," Gramma said, fussing with the wrap. "I just can't imagine where I'd wear something like this."

"Wear it in the house," Rachel said. Gramma gasped at the thought.

"I couldn't wear this in the house! The neighbors could see me and think I was being uppity." Gramma was always afraid someone would think she was being uppity. Dad reached under the tree for an oversize gift with Gramma's name on it.

"Then go on a cruise and wear it there," Dad said.

"Good Lord, Jack! What would the neighbors think if they knew I was on a cruise wearing this? Lorraine would never let me hear the end of it." Dad put the present at Gramma's feet.

"Isn't anybody else having Christmas around here?" she asked, tearing into the wrapping. She waded through layers of tissue paper before finding an envelope at the bottom of the box. She opened it and her mouth dropped open. "What in the world?" Rachel laughed and scooted next to her on the sofa.

"It's a ticket for a seven-day cruise." For once, Gramma sat speechless. "Aunt Kathy and Uncle Brian and everybody pitched in." Gramma held the ticket in front of her as if handling the Hope Diamond.

"I can't go on a cruise by myself," she whispered.

"Lorraine's going with you," Rachel said. Dad opened the door, and Lorraine cha-cha'd her way through the living room, wearing a bright red sweat suit with a big smiling reindeer sequined to the back. Gramma laughed and sprang to her feet, grabbing Lorraine's hands in midair. They laughed and cried like young girls on their wedding day, planning when to go and what to wear. Watching them, I was grateful Meghan had made me come.

Robert Layton picked the phone up in his home office and dialed a number. "Paula, this is Robert." Paula Hurley had worked at the local paper for as long as Robert could remember. Her father, John Hurley, owned the farm that Robert's parents visited every year with Robert and his brother in tow as they searched for the perfect Christmas tree.

"It's Christmas Day, Robert. Don't tell me you need a favor today."

"I need a favor today."

"What is it?"

"I need you to look up a fifteen-year-old obituary for me for a woman named Margaret Elizabeth Andrews."

“Don’t tell me you’ve got a client who’s suing the dead.”

“Nope. I think I just found an old friend.”

I shoved the last of the wrapping paper and empty boxes that covered the floor into a garbage bag and was about to take it out the back door when the doorbell rang. A man around my father’s age stood on the front porch wearing a brown leather jacket and holding a piece of paper in his hand. I assumed he was one of Dad’s customers. I opened the storm door to speak with him.

“Are you Nathan?” I told him I was and motioned for him to come in. He stood at the door and looked at me before extending his hand.

“My name is Robert Layton. I think you and I know each other.” When he heard a man’s voice, Dad walked into the living room, and I thought for sure he would take over from there; but Dad looked at the man as if he’d also never seen him before. “I’m Robert Layton,” he said again, shaking my father’s hand. “I don’t mean to disturb you but I wanted to be sure to catch someone at home and I was hoping it would be you,” he said, looking at me. Gramma and Rachel walked into the living room, and Robert did his introduction for the third and final time. “I don’t mean to interrupt your Christmas, so I’ll make this quick. This is going to sound strange, but I met Nathan fifteen years ago at Wilson’s Department Store.”

My mind raced through the employees at Wilson's. "I bought him a pair of sparkly shoes." Gramma threw her hand over her mouth. I was stunned. Even as a child I remembered a man had bought the shoes for me, but I could never picture his face. I only remember grabbing the shoes and running.

"That was you," I said. "How did you find me?" He held up the piece of paper.

"We met again at the cemetery." In my mind I could see Robert holding the wreath and poinsettias. "I didn't know it was you until I was leaving and the shoes on top of your mother's tombstone caught my eye. I wrote down the information and called a friend at the newspaper. I hope that wasn't too intrusive but I'd let you get away one Christmas. I didn't want it to happen again." A small tear fell down my grandmother's cheek.

"Days after Maggie died Nathan told us how he got those shoes," she said in a whisper. "You showed up at that store just like an angel." Robert smiled and cleared his throat, laughing.

"I wasn't an angel, believe me. I was on the verge of losing my family when I saw Nathan that Christmas Eve." We were captivated as Robert told us the story of his marriage to Kate and about his two girls. Kate had told him that the marriage was over. Robert was in Wilson's that night buying gifts for the last Christmas they'd spend together as a family. "It changed my life when I met you. I still can't explain it. All I know is that nothing mattered

to me more at that moment than my family, so I threw everything down and went home to my wife and kids—really went home for the first time in years." He stopped and cleared his throat again. "Anyway, I just wanted to thank you." He grabbed hold of me and wrapped his arms around me, pounding my back.

"Whose grave were you visiting?" I asked.

"My mother died that year, too—the day after Christmas. Christmas was her favorite time of year, so I decorate her grave no matter how cold it is, then I put a poinsettia on my father's grave. He didn't like decorations nearly as much as she did!"

Gramma told him how I had given the shoes to my mother that night. "Nathan was so proud," she said. "He put the shoes on Maggie's feet, and when her face lit up, Nathan just about burst, he was so happy. It's something I'll never forget." Dad jumped up to serve Robert a cup of coffee before we all dissolved into a puddle of tears. Gramma and Rachel went to clean the kitchen, leaving Robert and me alone. I noticed Robert's BMW parked on the side of the road.

"I bet you love that car," I said, pointing toward the window.

"That's only the second one I've owned. I had one the year my mother died, and I finally sold it six years ago. She did a lot of riding with me in that car, and I guess I had a hard time getting rid of it." I asked about Robert's work. "It's just a small practice," he said. "There was a

time when I had dreams of owning a huge practice; you know, fourteen floors of associates and partners with a penthouse office overlooking the river. Now that dream seems absurd." He came equipped with pictures of his grandson, and several of Kate and their two daughters and son-in-law. Robert was obviously a man in love with his family. "I blew it for a lot of years," he said, rifling through the pictures. We touched on everything from football (he was a diehard Giants fan), to cable television: "Eighty-seven channels, and I can't find anything to watch!" He shuffled the pictures around; one of his mother landed on top.

"What do you miss most about your mother?" He didn't need to think about the answer.

"Her presence." He put the pictures back into an envelope. "I miss her presence to this day. Months after she died I was still picking up the phone to call her, or I'd catch myself driving to her house."

"I remember getting off the school bus and running into the house. I'd always run straight to the kitchen for something to eat. Sometimes she'd be in there, already making dinner, but other times she'd be doing laundry or be in the back changing Rachel's diaper. I never really knew what she was doing; I just knew she was there; she was in the house. After she died I'd come home from school and wander around the house, trying to feel her again."

"But you couldn't."

"No."

“At the cemetery you told me you’re studying medicine,” he said. I didn’t remember telling him that. I made the conversation quick and told him I had just finished my last few days of school because it felt like the right thing to do. “You know, I love my job, but there are mornings when I sure don’t feel like talking with another client. After I saw you on Christmas Eve I felt a passion for my family that I hadn’t known in years but I didn’t *feel* in love with Kate and I knew she didn’t feel in love with me. If we were going to save our marriage we had to fuel up with something more than just feelings because the only ones we had between us were bitterness, anger, resentment, hostility, disappointment—feel free to stop me anytime.” I laughed along with him. “All I’m saying is, you may feel different in a while, so don’t pack it all in based on feelings alone.” Robert was a man I wished I had known my whole life; and in a way it felt as if I had. I looked at Robert and knew he believed what he was saying.

“Do you have a girlfriend at school?” he asked. “I’m just wondering what she thinks.” I looked down at my watch; I needed to go but for some reason I wanted to tell Robert everything about Meghan. I spoke quickly; there wasn’t much time; it was already seven-thirty. I told him about the scholarship race she was organizing and recognition of some kind registered on his face, but Robert only nodded, letting me ramble on till he was certain I had finished.

We exchanged phone numbers with promises to stay in touch. "All of you need to meet Kate. I know she'd love to have all of you over for dinner one night."

I walked Robert to the door and shook his hand. He had parked on the street and I watched as he got into his car and backed it into our driveway. My eyes fell to the license plate: L8N LAW. He drove away, and I closed the door.

ELEVEN

When I stand before God at the end of my life, I would hope that I would not have a single bit of talent left, and could say, "I used everything you gave me."
—Erma Bombeck

I pulled on my coat to leave for the hospital when the phone rang. It was eight o'clock. There are moments in life when you know who's going to be on the other end of a phone and what they're going to say and it's in that split second that you want to run. My foot was on the first step when my father stopped me. I looked at him. It was the same face I remember fifteen years ago when he told me my mother died. Dad ran to the truck and drove me to the hospital. He got there faster than I ever had.

In the course of only a few hours, Meghan's condition was deteriorating.

An hour earlier Dr. Goetz walked through the doors of the ICU and found Meghan's room. He stood at her side and brushed her cheek with the back of his hand. "You shouldn't have come in," she said. "It's Christmas."

“Do you think I’m going to let somebody else spend Christmas with my best girl?”

Meghan looked up at him. “Thank you, Dr. Goetz. Thank you for taking care of me for so long.” He smiled and patted her hand. “I know what’s happening.” Dr. Goetz felt his heart quicken; it was the same feeling he had experienced throughout the years when a patient knew that what happened next was beyond the scope of medicine and technology.

“They’re going to increase the antibiotics, Meghan, and . . .” She held firm to his hand.

“Will you tell my parents, Dr. Goetz?” She searched his eyes looking for truth, a recognition that he knew there was nothing more anyone could do. “Will you tell them what we know?”

Meghan opened her eyes and saw both her parents at her side. “I always knew what I had,” she whispered. Allison stroked her face and put her ear closer to Meghan.

“What?”

“I always knew what I had. I always knew I was loved.” Jim leaned forward and kissed her face. “I always knew you loved each other. So many kids never know that.” Allison held on to Meghan’s hand, letting her tears fall between her lips. “If we hadn’t moved to this part of town I never would have run, or met Charlie or Nathan. That move was the best thing that could have happened.

Remember, you always told me that?" Allison nodded. Meghan looked at her dad and squeezed his hand.

"Remind Mom that it's okay to be sad for a while, but not forever." He struggled to smile and kissed her again. "I love you, Daddy. I always knew that there was no place on earth that you'd rather be than with us." Jim picked up her hand and kissed it again and again.

"You are the gift we always prayed for," he said, stroking her cheek. "You are more than we ever imagined." He looked at Allison. "A lot of people throw the word 'grace' around but they don't really know what it means. I saw it in your eyes every time you looked at me, and I hear it in your mother's voice when she lies down next to me every night and says she loves me. I never deserved any of you, but God gave you to me anyway."

"I know you always thought that you were nothing, Daddy—that you were just some guy who worked in a garage, but you were everything to me." Jim leaned down and pulled her to him.

"I'm not going to say good-bye," Jim said, his tears falling onto Meghan's shoulders. "I'm going to keep holding you and never say good-bye."

"Show the stars to Luke and Olivia, Dad," Meghan said. "Olivia will get bored but show them to her anyway." Meghan pulled away from her father and reached for Allison. "Tell them I love them, Mom. Will you tell them over and over for me?" Allison smiled and smoothed Meghan's hair. "And when Olivia asks why

I'm not home, will you help her understand?" Tears streamed down Allison's face as she nodded.

When I got to the hospital, Meghan was sleeping. I walked to her bedside and looked at her face; she was beautiful, too beautiful to believe she was ill. I held her hand and kissed it, holding it to my face.

This is why Dr. Goetz left medicine, I thought, looking at her. *And this is why he came back.*

Meghan opened her eyes and smiled.

"How was your family?" she said. Her voice was getting weak.

"I never should have gone." She held up her hand.

"Yes, you should have. Tell me how it was." I sat down and told her about Gramma's gift and how she and Lorraine acted like young girls again and Meghan smiled. She wanted to hear more so I told her about Robert and her eyes widened.

"That's the miracle, Nathan!" I couldn't imagine what she meant. "Robert came back into your life on Christmas. I told you there's always a Christmas miracle." Her eyes were dancing; she wanted nothing more than to convince me. "That's why you were supposed to be with your family today. If you hadn't gone, you would have missed your miracle."

"But what about your miracle, Meg?" She put her hand on my face.

"I have my miracle."

I shook my head.

"It was your love for me, Nathan. I couldn't leave without falling in love, so God brought you to me." A tear ran down my face. It was a heartbreaking, yet beautiful thought: Somehow, out of all the men in the world, I was chosen to love this extraordinary woman. "He brought you to me because you know how to love people, Nathan. You know how to care." My mother's letter sprang to my mind: *The pain you feel now will help you care for others*. Meghan ran her hand down the side of my face. "That's why you were meant to be a doctor. Because you listen from here." She touched my chest, resting her hand over my heart. "You were meant to work with children because they need people to listen to them from here. Not everyone can do that, but you can. It's your gift." She squeezed my hand and smiled; it was still the prettiest smile I'd ever seen. I tried to speak but felt a knot in my throat. She lifted her hand to stop me.

"You take the good with the bad. It's all part of the package. Remember?" I leaned down and held her face next to mine, feeling her breath on my cheek. *Please let her live,* I prayed. *Oh God, please don't let this happen.* We talked for as long as we could before Meghan grew tired and closed her eyes. Jim and Allison stood beside me and we watched her breathe, and waited. It was the only thing left to do.

• • •

It was a few minutes before eleven when Dr. Goetz ran into Meghan's room and told us a liver was available. Seconds later two orderlies came into the room and pushed Meghan's bed down the hall. The room was spinning; everything was happening so fast. We ran into the hall, prepared to follow the orderlies who were pushing Meghan to the OR, but Dr. Goetz stopped us. He told us about Meghan's donor: It was the miracle Meghan had been holding on to but it came at such a price.

It was late on Christmas night, and Charlie was on the sofa with Rich flipping through the picture book of Alaska he had unwrapped that morning. Charlie had already looked through it several times but was now going through it page by page with Rich. "Tell me about Alaska, Dad."

"Which part?"

"All of it. I want to hear about the birds with the colorful bills that sit on the water and about the dolphins and whales and the mountains. All of it."

"But we're going to go there someday, then you'll see it all for yourself."

"Tell me now, Dad," he said, whispering. "Tell me now so I can see it." Rich wrapped his arm around Charlie and pulled him closer, resting Charlie's head on his shoulder, and began to tell him one story after another till Charlie closed his eyes and slept. Death was quiet when it came

that night. Several minutes into his story, Rich heard Charlie's breathing stop and screamed for Leslie. They called for an ambulance, but knew it was too late. His heart had stopped. Looking back, I was amazed at the strength my father and grandmother had as my mother was dying. Grieving parents were granted that same strength when they needed it most. An indescribable peace surrounded Rich and Leslie as they held on to Charlie, kissing him and thanking him for being their son.

Somehow, in the middle of their grief, Rich and Leslie made it known that Charlie wanted his liver to be tested to see if it could be a match for Meghan and that he wanted any of his healthy organs to help anyone who needed them. At first, Rich thought Charlie's liver might have been damaged from medications, but it was healthy and as close to an ideal match as possible.

We would not tell Meghan about Charlie until well after the transplant. It was an indescribable, bittersweet miracle that left all of us conflicted with feelings of loss and joy, grief and hope.

Soon after my mother died, my grandmother scribbled something on a pink notepad and taped it to her bathroom mirror. I read it again and again when I was a boy, never fully comprehending it. It read, *Now we see but a poor reflection as in a mirror; then we shall see face-to-face. Now I know in part; then I shall know fully . . . And now these three remain: faith, hope, and love. But the greatest of these is love.* It was the longer look my grandmother had tried to tell me about. One day we'd know everything, but for now we would live with so many unanswered questions.

It was Love that came down on Christmas, my mother said. *That is the greatest miracle of all. That is the blessing of Christmas.* It is love that requires us to do the hardest thing in impossible situations. It was love that compelled Rich and Leslie Bennett to think of someone else's life during their greatest tragedy.

My heart broke for Rich and Leslie, for Meghan, and for all of us who had been touched by Charlie's life. *How could Rich and Leslie think of someone else as they held Charlie in their arms?* But I knew. Of course I knew: *And now these three remain: faith, hope, and love. But the greatest of these is love.*

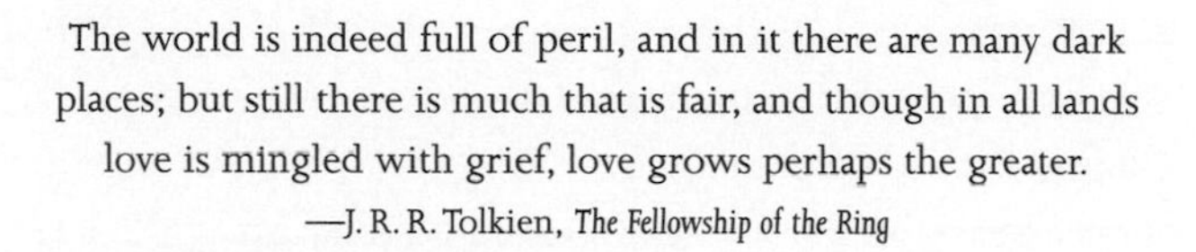

TWELVE

The world is indeed full of peril, and in it there are many dark places; but still there is much that is fair, and though in all lands love is mingled with grief, love grows perhaps the greater.

—J. R. R. Tolkien, *The Fellowship of the Ring*

I heard a knock on the door and opened it to see William. "Turn on the news," he said, brushing past me. He flipped on the television, and I sat on the sofa. Footage of Meghan winning a race in early fall was playing. I flipped to another channel and that station was running a story about her and Charlie as well. "How do you explain your ability to run so fast?" the reporter asked after a race. Meghan threw her arm over Michele's shoulder.

"I don't really know, but I think we've all been given something, you know? Some sort of gift that we're supposed to unwrap and give away. I think running was my gift." I leaned my head on the back of the sofa, listening to her.

"And how could you give that away?" the reporter asked. Meghan was embarrassed, and she looked down at the ground.

“I want to raise money for pediatric heart patients and help them go to college. I know it’s nothing huge but I hope it can help in a small way because even the smallest ripple can change the shape of water.” She squinted as she looked toward the camera. The reporter spoke of the scholarship race Meghan had been organizing and showed some of the tiny heart patients at the hospital. Pictures of Charlie flashed on the screen, and the reporter spoke about their friendship. I sat up and watched them replay the tape of Meghan running across the finish line, smiling.

William went with me to the funeral. We drove to the church but had to park several blocks away. We walked in silence with the rest of the crowd and saw Dr. Goetz helping his wife out of their car. William and I walked into the church together, which overflowed with members of the church, along with Meghan’s team, who loved Charlie. They all wore running suits in honor of his relationship with them. Denise and Claudia and several of the pediatrics staff members sat in a row together. William and I sat a few rows behind Jim, Luke, and Olivia. Allison stayed with Meghan in the hospital. Charlie’s teacher spoke at his funeral, along with Dr. Goetz and the minister. Charlie would have been embarrassed at the fuss everyone was making. I could see him cracking his knuckles in nervous anticipation of the whole thing just being over and done.

William and I stepped outside the church at the end of the service and the wind shrieked when I opened the door. I felt a little hand grab mine, and I looked down to see Olivia.

"It's so cold, Olivia," I said, leading her toward the door. "Why don't you go back inside?"

"My mom says Charlie isn't here. She said he's already in Heaven."

"That's right." The wind picked up her hair, and she closed her eyes. I pulled the hood of her coat over her head.

"Did God take Charlie to Heaven so Meghan could live?"

I sat down on the top step so I could look at her. "No," I said, remembering the words my mother had said to me. "God didn't take Charlie to Heaven. He received him: There's a big difference." She looked at me, trying to understand what I was saying. "Life took Charlie away from us."

"Why?"

"Because he was human."

After the funeral, I drove to my father's house, but he, Rachel, and Gramma weren't home. I noticed photo albums and the box of letters strewn on top of my grandmother's bed. It looked as if she was in the middle of cleaning out her closet. I sat on the bed and started rifling through the albums. There is a distinct break in one of the albums: The pictures go from the entire family together to ones that no longer include my mother. The rest of that album took over three years to fill. I reached for a letter that was sitting on top of another photo album and instead of discarding it back to the pile I opened it, recognizing my handwriting as a teenager:

Dear Mom,
I often wonder how those doctors treated you when you went to the hospital for tests. I wonder how they made you feel. Did they scare you or were they good to you, sitting by your side and making you feel safe? I wonder if they took the time to talk and get to know you. I wonder if they ever knew what a great mom you were or how you could make Dad laugh. I wonder if they felt bad when you passed away, or if they even knew. I wonder if they realized what the world missed when you died?

I miss you and love you every day,
Nathan

I held on to the letter as tears blurred my vision. It contained the reasons why I wanted to become a physician: Not because I thought I could save everyone but because I wanted each patient to know that he or she was being cared for to the very end. It was what my mother had tried to teach me before she died—the pain of living without her would help me care for others. It wasn't a weakness as I had thought for so long; it was my gift. Just as Meghan said.

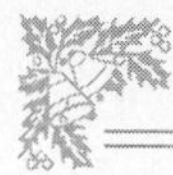

THIRTEEN

You gain strength, courage and confidence by every experience in which you really stop to look fear in the face. . . .
You must do the thing you think you cannot do.
—Eleanor Roosevelt

Robert Layton cradled his grandson, Evan, with one arm and picked the phone up in his den with the other. He dialed a number written in his personal address book. "Allen," Robert said, bouncing Evan up and down. "Are you still in the Christmas spirit?" Robert hung up the phone, wrote something on a legal pad, and dialed the next number. "Larry, this is Robert. I need your help." After several phone calls, Robert went to the kitchen and fixed a bottle for Evan.

"I can take him, Dad," his daughter Hannah said. Robert held the baby away from her.

"Don't even think about taking him. He's Grandpa's buddy." Robert stuck the warm bottle in Evan's mouth. "Aren't you Grandpa's buddy?" He whispered in the baby's ear. "Come on, let's get back to work." He slipped back inside his den.

"What are you working on in there, Dad?" Hannah said.

"Top-secret stuff," Robert said, holding the phone to his ear. "Gray, it's Robert Layton." He yelled into the phone. "Robert Layton! Can you hear me? Good. Do you have a second, Gray? I need your help with something." When Kate heard Robert shouting she stuck her head inside the den. He saw her and waved his hand, shooing her away.

He hung up the receiver, jotted something on his legal pad, and smiled before picking up the phone again.

I showered and reached toward the bathroom counter for the watch my mother had given me. I paused, then picked it up and looked at the time; it was running ten minutes behind. I didn't tap the face of it, but flipped it over to the inscription on the back: *With all the love in the world, Mom.* I ran my finger over the inscription and pulled out a piece of paper from my backpack and sat down at the table and began writing:

Dear Mom,

I think it's time to put away the watch you gave me. It doesn't mean I don't love you; it just means it's time to move on.

With all the love in the world,

Nathan

I put the watch and letter next to a picture of my mother and me on top of the chest of drawers and reached for the watch Meghan had given me. I put it on and finished dressing. My time at the hospital was done, but I went there anyway and lingered around a closed office door.

Dr. Goetz arrived a few minutes later with a cup of coffee in his hand. "Come on in," he said, unlocking the door. He looked tired; it had been a rough week. He offered me a seat, and I sat down, unzipping my coat. I knew he was wondering why I was there.

"Do patients know they're dying?"

"Some of them do."

"Do you think he knew?"

"I think he always knew. That's why he lived the way he did."

"Do you ever get used to it?"

He leaned back in his chair and sighed, looking at the ceiling. "No." He looked at me. "But you learn to accept it." He was quiet. "Sometimes it's just harder to accept."

Though I had gone over what I wanted to say several times in my head, I found myself stammering for the right words. "I would like to be part of your rotation again."

Dr. Goetz stirred his coffee and stared at me.

"Why?"

I had a feeling this wasn't going to be as easy as I'd hoped. "Because someone recently told me that you need to run with somebody better than you." Dr. Goetz smiled; he understood the reference. "That if I want to be the best, I have to run with the best." He sipped his coffee.

"That's good advice."

"Someone else said that we need to keep our eyes on the goal . . . if we take our eyes off the goal, we'll never make it to the end." He swallowed hard and looked at me, studying my face.

"It's not going to be any easier."

"I know that."

"What makes you think you can stick it out this time?"

"Because I can't just leave. If I could walk away, I would; but I'd never be happy." He leaned back and studied my face. I knew he believed me. "And, to answer your question . . . medicine is a calling." He nodded, and I could see the corners of his mouth turn up just a bit.

"There are things that I cannot tolerate from med students, Mr. Andrews. If you arrive late for a rotation, that shows me that . . ." I held up my wrist, stopping him.

"That will never happen again. I have a new watch." He smiled and cleared his throat. "Dr. Goetz, I need to apologize to you because I've made a lot of mistakes and—"

"So, are you here to waste my morning by telling me all the mistakes you've made, or are you here to start over?"

"I'd like to start over," I said, smiling.

. . .

Denise looked inside Meghan's room. Meghan had been moved out of ICU only days earlier into the step-down unit. "People are calling from all over about the scholarship run," Denise said, holding on to paperwork. "Two separate law firms alone have donated $5000 each." Jim and Allison sat in silence, listening. "Just within the last several days, $25,000 has been donated." Meghan gasped. Allison threw her hands over her face and cried. The scholarship fund would be bigger than what Meghan had ever dreamed.

My mind recalled a piece of conversation I had had with Meghan. "Some attorney in Jefferson gave $500," she said. *Could Robert Layton be that attorney?* I followed Denise into the hallway and looked over the donation sheets—there it was, Layton and Associates for $500. I called him, and Robert asked me to bring Dad and Gramma to his house that weekend for dinner.

When we arrived, Kate opened the door. She was a beautiful woman. I could see why Robert fell for her nearly thirty years ago. She threw open her arms and wrapped them around me. "You really do exist." Kate was as accessible in spirit as Robert. "For so many years I wondered what happened to you," she said to me. "Now look at you, sitting in our house and looking back at me!" Robert walked in through the garage door carrying an armful of firewood. Dad jumped up to help.

"Sit down, Jack," Kate said, springing to her feet.

"You're our guest. Robert can get it." Robert grunted as he bent to the floor, easing the wood into the bin on the hearth.

"When a man's arms are breaking, Kate, and another man offers to help . . . let him help." He greeted all of us with a hug, then said, "Can I bring out some hors d'oeuvres and drinks for everybody?" Kate moved toward the kitchen to help.

"Let me help with that," I said, following Robert into the kitchen. I wanted to ask Robert about the law firms and businesses that had donated money to the run, but didn't know how to bring it up.

"How's Meghan today?" he asked.

"She's great. Doctors see improvement every day."

"Does she know about Charlie?"

"Her mom and dad and Charlie's parents told her about a week after the funeral. She didn't take the news very well. How could she?" Robert didn't say anything. There was nothing anyone could ever say. I looked at Robert and tried to think of a way to ask him about the donations to the scholarship run. He gave me an opening.

"What's up?" he said.

"There's been this outpouring of donations for Meghan's scholarship run from lawyers and companies that the hospital hasn't heard of, people the Sullivans don't even know." Robert was listening with interest; he knew I was on to him. "It seems that someone is doing some staggering fund-raising for this run." Robert was nonchalant, impressed only with the scholarship run itself.

"Probably a friend of hers who wants to help."

"It seems to me that this *friend* is someone the Sullivans don't know, someone they've never met." Robert pulled glasses from the cupboard and began filling them with ice. "The Sullivans are trying to come up with a name for the race. I thought maybe they should name it after the person who's been so influential in fund-raising, what do you think?" Robert replaced the ice bin to the freezer and smiled.

"I think they should call it whatever Meghan wants."

"But maybe people should know that someone else was responsible for . . ." He held up his hand, cutting me off.

"This is Meghan's gift to someone. She should be the one giving it away." I watched him fill the glasses with ice before asking him what had been on my mind for so long.

"How'd you ever donate to the run in the first place?"

"She called my office one day and my assistant walked to my desk and said I should take the call. I knew it was important to Jodie; she's a runner, so when Meghan asked for a donation, I couldn't refuse that sweet voice."

"The Sullivans are going to need help with the money. They need someone to walk them through setting up a trust or something." Robert nodded.

"I know a few firms who would be glad to help. I'll

have Jodie get a package of info to you on each firm, and you can pass it on to the Sullivans."

There are some people who go through life seizing whatever they can for themselves; then there are others who, once their lives are touched, cannot help but leave others changed as well. Robert was such a person. No one would ever know who was working so hard behind the scenes for Meghan's run, and somehow that suited Robert just fine. Meghan was right: Robert's coming back into my life was one of the small miracles of Christmas.

I spoke with Robert's assistant about the package of info he'd pulled together for the Sullivans. "It's ready," Jodie said. "How do you want me to get it to you?"

"I can just swing by and pick it up."

"That'll be out of your way, though. Where do you live? Are you close to the university?"

"I live on the property, but it can be confusing for someone who's not used to all these little streets."

"I have to drive by Bryan Park on my way home every day. Do you know where that is?" We agreed to meet in the park at the end of the workday. I drove around the parking lot looking for anyone sitting in a car, but when I couldn't spot anyone I parked my truck and watched people ice-skating on the lake.

The runner with the neon ball cap made her way around the lake as I waited. I thought about getting out

and talking with her, but I didn't want to miss Jodie, and since I saw this woman running here so often, I knew I'd get another chance. A car pulled in beside me, but a mother and her two young children got out and toted their ice skates down the hill toward the lake. Meghan's runner made another lap around the lake before she slowed down and walked the hill toward the cars. She banged her hands together and pulled the cap farther down on her head, swinging her arms. She caught me watching her, and I looked away, fidgeting with the buttons on my stereo. I jumped when I heard a small rap on my window. I looked up and saw the neon cap. I rolled the window down and looked at her, wondering what she wanted. "Are you Nathan?" *How did she know my name?* "Are you Robert's friend?"

"Are *you* Jodie?" I whispered.

"I am." She extended her hand through the window. "Nice to meet you." I reached up, grabbed her hand, and pumped it up and down, laughing.

FOURTEEN

Where there is great love, there are always miracles.

—Willa Cather

In June, hundreds of runners lined up in front of the courthouse. A banner stretched high above the street, THE CHARLIE BENNETT SCHOLARSHIP RUN—Meghan wouldn't consider naming the run after herself. Hospital administrators and medical staff were out in force wearing matching yellow T-shirts with the name of the run on the front and the name of the department they worked in on the back. Denise and Claudia were busy corralling the pediatrics department, who were the noisiest by far. Dr. Goetz held on to a streetlight and stretched his quadriceps. "Don't fail me now," he said each time he stretched a muscle. "Just get me through this and I promise I'll take better care of you."

Dad, along with Lydia, Gramma, Rachel, and Lorraine (wearing a leopard-print sweat suit—she must have thought the print would at least make her look fast) lined up next to William, Robert and Kate, and Jodie, who was sporting her neon ball cap, of course.

“I’ll stay with you, Gramma,” Rachel said.

“Don’t be ridiculous. You run alongside your father and Lydia. Lorraine and I will stick together and walk across the finish line at midnight if we have to.”

“Midnight,” Lorraine shouted. “You didn’t say anything about being out here till midnight!” Gramma turned to her in a flash.

“We’ll stay out here till dawn if we have to, Lorraine!”

“Well, I can’t walk far, Evelyn. My knees will never let me.”

“There’s nothing wrong with your knees, and everybody knows it, Lorraine!” Lorraine stuck her hands in the jacket of her sweat suit and pouted, wishing she’d never answered the phone that morning.

I felt arms around my waist and looked down at Olivia; she was looking more like Meghan every day. Jim pushed Meghan through the crowd in a wheelchair. It was the only way doctors would let her participate. It would be well over a year before she would run again.

Earlier in the morning we had gone to Bryan Park, and Jim and I unloaded a bench from the back of my truck and set it under the oak tree by the lake. Rich and Leslie were there along with my family. Meghan tried to speak but couldn’t. Every time she thought of Charlie she cried, and the day of race was especially emotional. She gripped my hand and looked at me for help, but I didn’t need to say anything. Leslie read the plaque on the bench and tears flooded her eyes. It was for Charlie. Meghan had

agonized what to put on it; she wanted it to reflect not only her heart, but Charlie's as well. It read:

IN MEMORY OF CHARLIE BENNETT
THE GREATEST MIRACLE OF ALL IS THE
LOVE OF A TRUE FRIEND

"I just wish I could thank him," Meghan whispered, holding on to Leslie.

"He knows," Leslie said, wiping tears from her face.

Jim pushed Meghan to the front of the line, and someone handed her a microphone. She welcomed the runners to the first annual Charlie Bennett Scholarship Run, then paused. I didn't know if she could get through the few words she wanted to say. "Many of you know that I am blessed to be here today," she said. "But I am more blessed to have called Charlie Bennett my friend." She put the microphone on her lap and paused. She had more to say but couldn't. She lifted the microphone to her mouth. "Let's run this for him," she said. She fired the starter's gun into the air, and the university band struck up a tune as the runners took off, running Meghan's dream.

We wound our way through town and into Bryan Park. Leslie had pushed her to the spot where we had positioned Charlie's bench earlier in the morning. They sat there together watching one runner after another make their way around the lake. I ran around it several

times, just so I could kiss Meghan and see that pretty smile. I ran onto the path again with the other runners and grabbed Olivia's hand as the sun made its way from behind the clouds and shimmered off the water.

"Look at that," Olivia said, pointing to the water. "Heaven just opened up, and Charlie's smiling." Somehow, I think she was right.

I watched people cross the finish line, one by one, and I smiled, thinking of what Meghan told me while she sat in the cab of my truck—she had indeed changed her small part of the world. The money raised that day was $100,000, more than anything she had ever imagined.

EPILOGUE

. . . let us run with perseverance the race marked out for us.

—Paul of Tarsus

The wind has picked up, spraying a fine powder of snow along the lake's edge. Carolers are inside the gazebo warming up for a brief concert this evening. I stabilize the bench and shine the plaque that reads, *For Meghan Sullivan and all who believe in miracles.* I take a seat and look out over the frozen water. It is nice to see that the park hasn't changed in the three years I have been away, and the grounds are still beautiful, even in December. During the past four years, I finished up my fourth year of medical school with Dr. Goetz, then went to Rainbow Babies and Children's Hospital in Cleveland for three years of residency. I have moved back into town to take two months off before heading to Boston's Children's Hospital for three years of fellowship training in pediatric cardiology, keeping me closer to home. Then, hopefully, I'll come back and work in the hospital's cardiology department for a few years with Dr. Goetz before he retires.

Meghan went back to school on a part-time basis the fall after her transplant, but she chose not to go to Stanford or Georgetown; she stayed at the university and when she was able, she ran for them, "helping to put us on the map," as Michele Norris said. Meghan studied education with the hopes of teaching and coaching. She will be unbelievable at both.

Ice-skaters laugh as they attempt to make figure eights on the frozen lake. Two little girls, who look no older than three, run from the lake and climb up on Charlie's bench; the tassels on their knit hats bounce up and down. They look at me, and I see that they're twins. "Hi," one of them says.

"Hi."

"What are you doing?" the other little girl asks.

"Just leaving a bench here."

"For who?"

"For Meghan Sullivan." Their eyes light up.

"Our brother knew her," one of them says. I assume their brother was on one of the teams at the university. "He went to Heaven when she got her new liver." I snap my head to look at them. They are Rich and Leslie's twins. Soon after Charlie died, Leslie discovered she was pregnant. They had never planned for more children, so the news surprised them, to say the least. On what would have been Charlie's thirteenth birthday, Rich and Leslie laid flowers on his grave and Leslie felt one of the babies kick for the first time.

“That little kick brought such light to such a dark day,” Leslie later said to Meghan. “These little girls brought nothing but joy with them when they were born.” I watch them and see what she means. They are adorable, much cuter than the pictures I’ve seen.

“Come on, we need to get going,” I hear someone say behind me. I turn to see a young man behind me who can’t be older than fourteen but already he is as tall as I am. He motions for the girls to come to him. I look at him and can see the resemblance: the eyes, the nose, the jawline—it is Matthew, Charlie’s brother. “Do you need help?” he asks me.

“No. Thank you.” During the brief time I knew Charlie, I only met Matthew once, but he was a little boy. He doesn’t remember who I am, and I had no idea he would have grown so much in four years. I open my mouth to tell him what an incredible person his brother was.

“I’m supposed to meet our parents in a few minutes, and I have to get them out of these clothes or else my mom will kill me,” he says. I smile. They are headed to the same place I am. I shake his hand, and the little girls wave.

“Hey, what’s your name,” one of them asks, turning around.

“Nathan. What’s yours?”

“I’m Abigail and she’s Allie.”

“Both of those names sound like the name of a princess. Are both of you princesses?”

“I am,” Abigail says. “She’s not.” I laugh and look

down at Charlie's bench. I often wonder if he ran through the gates of Heaven like he wanted to. I smile. *He did. I know he did.*

During my training, there have been other children who have died since Charlie; children who entered my life for only the shortest time; but they have taught me, like my mother said, it's not about how long you live, but how you live, because before you know it, our time is up and we leave this place. Each of their lives was too short, but they all left their small part of the world changed, leaving this physician with the desire to be a better person, to change the shape of water; but to do that I have to jump into the water first. It's what my mother wanted me to learn.

I jump in the truck and drive through town, parking at the side of the road. I run inside the back of the building, and my grandmother and Rachel hurry to fix my tie. Tears are in their eyes as they kiss my cheek. "Thought you were AWOL there for a minute," Dad says, grinning. Lydia squeezes my arm. She and my father have been married nearly a year now and are very happy together. Lydia is a wonderful woman. She loves my grandmother; they cook together and go for walks and every now and then Lydia will sit down with Gramma and Lorraine and watch the Atlanta Braves play. She's even learned how to antagonize Lorraine, booing the Braves and cheering for the Indians during my time in Cleveland. For the first time in my life, Lorraine is wearing a skirt and jacket, not

a sweat suit with sneakers, and there are no sequins in sight.

"No sweat suit, Lorraine?" I ask.

"I'm not trash, doll," she says, her laughter shaking the rafters.

Dad and I walk down the aisle toward the front, which has been decorated with red and white poinsettias and a Christmas tree covered with sparkling lights, gold ribbon, and red bulbs. Swags of spruce held together with strings of holly berries hang between each pew. As I pass, I smile at Robert and Kate, Dr. Goetz, Hope, who is now nine and beautiful, the Sullivans and the Bennetts, with Matthew and the twins at their side. The girls look at me, and their mouths open wide. One jumps on Rich's lap and begins to tell him something, but Leslie shushes her, fussing with her hair. I smile at them and take my place at the front, Dad by my side, along with William, who's flown in from his residency in Texas.

It's been twenty years since I stood on that windy hillside with my mother. "*Time in the valley will teach you to be a man, Nathan,*" she had said. "*It's where your character will form. I hope you go through the valley so that you'll learn how to love and feel and understand. And when life wounds you, I hope it is because you loved people, not because you mistreated them.*" It was a blessing of sorts; a blessing that forges love in the darkest places.

There have been times, especially during those early years without her, that I thought time in the valley was anything but a blessing, but now I know otherwise. As I

grew, I began to understand what my mother meant: It is those times of struggle and pain that teach us how to live. It's not really living until you've thrown your heart and soul on the line, risking failure and suffering loss. And I have come to realize that we're never alone; everyone has been through their own valley or is walking through it now: A man fights alcoholism and vows his family won't live through the sickness and sadness of his own youth, a young woman contracts a disease and parents stand by her bedside praying for a miracle, spouses die, leaving brokenhearted widows or widowers behind, couples fight and separate, cars crash, a young boy dies, leaving a hole in the heart of everyone he touched. There were times when the grief in my life made it impossible to believe that God was alive and working, or the doubts were so great it seemed hopeless to believe anything at all, but as I look at the faces in the seats before me I know once again that we're all here for a reason, a purpose that is often beyond us.

The music swells, and I look up to see my bride standing at the back of the church. The wedding is small; many people couldn't make it into town for Christmas Eve. We knew that as we planned, but Meghan insisted we get married at Christmas, to honor both my mother and Charlie. "Even God's smallest plan is bigger than any dream we'll ever hope for," my father said, dragging our rowboat onto shore so many years ago. Glancing at him now, I still don't understand why God's plan couldn't

include saving my mother, or Charlie; I know I never will. I smile as Meghan walks down the aisle and can hear the twins clap and giggle when they see her.

But I know that although we may never understand it, there is a plan, and though it may be traced in pain, in the end there will be joy, and it will be beautiful.